TEA BISCUIT

Equestrian Fiction by Barbara Morgenroth

~ BITTERSWEET FARM 8 ~

TEA BISCUIT

Barbara Morgenroth

DashingBooks

ISBN: 978-0692332368

Cover photo by Bob Haarmans

Published by DashingBooks

Text set in Adobe Garamond

1

THE BARN PHONE BEGAN RINGING and since I was closest to the tack room, I went for it.

"Bittersweet Farm."

"This is Shawn Newton. May I speak to Lockie Malone?"

I didn't recognize the name but I didn't expect to know many people he knew. "I'll get him for you."

I went onto the aisle. "Lockie, phone for you."

Lockie led Wingspread from his stall and put him on the cross-ties. Wing was scheduled for a session in the indoor where simple gymnastics were the work of the day.

"Who is it?"

"Shawn Newton I think he said."

"Would you get Wing tacked for me? I'll be right there."

I nodded and we both went into the tack room, me for his saddle and Lockie to get the phone.

The weather had improved lately but while the snow had melted, we were left with mud. It was a difficult time of year when the ground couldn't firm up quickly enough. Everyone was ready for the winter to end and be able to ride outside without getting muddy to the knees. There were shows in our near future and most of them would be outside. I wasn't looking forward to parking in a field with four inches of squishy dirt covered with beige grass.

I was just buckling the girth when Lockie approached. "Get CB and we'll take a ride down the road."

When he looked like that and spoke in that tone of voice, I didn't question. Something serious was on his mind.

Lockie finished tacking Wing, and was leaving the barn by the time I clipped the cross-ties to CB's halter.

"I don't know what happened, but it's not good."

CB put his nose on my face and we breathed on each other for a moment, then I kissed him and brought him outside. I mounted and we walked to the indoor where Lockie was trotting.

They looked good. Wing's frame had elongated after focusing on that issue all winter and I thought he had as good as chance as any horse to go from eventing into the hunter division. Maybe he would never be as stretch and reach as was seen in the hunter under saddle classes, but

Wing did have a floating stride that covered ground without using too much energy.

Lockie looked up and pulled to a walk near us. "Let's go."

We rode in silence to the top of the driveway then turned right on the dirt road. It was damp but firm.

"Don't overreact," Lockie started.

"That's a terrible way to preface bad news."

"My friend, Tinker Devlin, preceded me to Germany and found a position in a large training facility."

"Eventing?"

"Yes. He had a bad fall today."

"How bad?" I asked but already knew.

Lockie was silent.

"You should attend the funeral."

"Yes."

"Do what you think is right. Take as much time as you need."

"He left me his horse."

"The one who fell with him?"

"That was a colt he was training."

I held out my hand to him. "I'm sorry."

He took my hand. "It's not often in the forefront of my mind, then something like this happens and I can't help but think it could have been me. It could have been me."

"I think that, too, all the time." I had more to say but this was not the right moment.

3

Lockie was fortunate Wing didn't fall with him, that he quit in the best way possible for the conditions. For months, I had blamed Wing, but had come to accept that it was an instantaneous calculation—he knew he couldn't make it over the berm with the footing so deep and slippery.

After trying to recreate the moment in my imagination, I still couldn't picture it clearly. I don't know why Lockie didn't break his nose on Wing's neck, but came off instead. That suggested to me that Wing couldn't have stopped, he had to have run out so there was nothing in front of Lockie and his body continued in the direction it had been going.

Lockie had no memory of the incident. If he had been told, he didn't remember that either.

It was an accident. If accident means the unexpected happens. Best leave it at that.

Predicting what a horse will do under all conditions wasn't possible. They had their own thoughts and emotions. They made their own choices, even if it was something as simple as CB's swish. He did that because he wanted to. The importance of a dressage competition was vital only to the rider, not the horse. If he won or lost made no difference. Having a cookie was important.

"Do you know his horse?" I asked.

"It's a dark bay gelding named Nassau."

"We have room."

"Talia, thank you for not freaking out."

4

"You're welcome."

Lockie looked at me. "But you're freaking out inside."

"We wouldn't recognize me if that wasn't true."

Lockie let my hand go and turned Wing. "You have your *Zuckerweurfel* this afternoon and I have to book a flight to Tink's home."

An hour later Greer came up to the main barn from her office. "Did Lockie ride Counterpoint?"

"No, I think he's all yours now."

"Will he be able to do a session after your ponies?"

I finished checking Call's leg, decided he was very sound and one of the girls should ride him for the lesson. "Lockie is at the carriage house and I don't know when he'll be back."

"Why?"

"A friend of his died in an accident today so he's..."

Greer shook her head. "I'll take the ponies. Go be with him."

"You can help with the ponies but he needs some time to himself."

"What happened to your Florence Nightingale mode? Why aren't you down there taking care of him?"

"My trying to take care of people is annoying."

"So?"

"You always...mocked me."

"Because I don't have what you have. And you know me, I can't express concern for anyone."

"Cam's father," I said.

"That's a first. I read with him because that's all I can do."

"I know that's not true."

"You care for people so easily. That's your gift. My gift is organizing." Greer smiled ruefully. "It's not much but it's what I have."

"That's such bull. You have so much to offer."

"What if I offered and was turned down. I've never been liked very well for me."

I put my arms around her. "That's the past. Cam likes you enough to fly up from Florida to help you."

Stepping away, Greer went to the tack room. "You put him in a position where he couldn't say no."

I followed her. "That's not true."

"He went to that charity event with Sloane Radclyffe."

The Scintillating Socialite. That was a big mistake on Cam's part. Greer would never forget that.

"He doesn't come to the barn." Greer took Counterpoint's bridle off the rack.

"Cam just got back from Florida. Give him a chance to catch up on things like...going to the dentist. I don't know what he's doing. It's not as though he's going to stay away forever. He has three horses here."

"Two!" She left the tack room

Greer would never give Remington back to him.

"Make it possible for Cam to..." I called after her.

"Do what?" Cam asked, stepping out of Whiskey's stall.

Greer had come to a halt in front of Counterpoint and looked to me for help.

"Go on a trail ride together," I finished.

"Yeah, good idea. It's time for Whisk to get back into work. You're getting on Counterpoint?"

Greer nodded. "I was."

"Good timing then," Cam replied.

What never ceased to amaze me was how good natured he was with her. Greer could be so difficult to deal with and she was particularly hard on him, yet Cam brushed it off every time.

I saw how Lockie trained the young horses who challenged him by being resistant to what he asked of them. Lockie rode past the behaviors, ignoring them, correcting them, if possible, and eventually getting to a place of cooperation.

It was probably better if I didn't point out to Greer that this was what Cam seemed to be doing with her. No one wants to think they're being handled. I thought she was lucky he was willing to put the time in on her but doubted if she'd agree. At least not immediately.

As I watched Cam and Greer leave on their hack, Poppy Beck arrived, excited as always. She gave me a big hug as she told me all about her school day and classmates I would never meet and couldn't keep straight.

"How would you like to have two lessons today, one on Call and one on Tango?"

Poppy jumped up and down. "Did you hear that, Mom? Isn't that awesome?"

Aly Beck smiled at me.

"And you can help with the afternoon chores, too, if your mother says you don't have to rush home."

"Please, Mom!"

Aly and I laughed. The simple pleasure of mucking stalls, and being considered responsible enough to work, had this young rider dancing in the aisle.

***

Jules was starting dinner when I entered the kitchen, needing a mug of tea and something delicious to carry me through chores.

"Is there anything to eat?" I asked washing my hands.

"Would you like bruschetta? I bought some fresh mozzarella today and can make you a little pizza."

"Hug first, food later," I said.

Jules wrapped her arms around me. "What's wrong?"

"A friend of Lockie was killed in an accident today and he's been at the carriage house all afternoon thinking about it."

"Why aren't you with him?"

"I thought he wanted to sort it out for himself." I put a mug of water in the microwave and turned it on. "I didn't know this friend since I know very few people from Lockie's past. He was an event rider. I'm guessing it was a rotational fall."

"Which is?"

"The horse hits the jump in a way that it flips over the fence. If the rider is thrown clear, they probably both walk away, sore but alive. If the rider winds up under the horse, it's a less pleasant outcome."

Jules turned on the grill and brought out the Tuscan bread she had made.

"I know it doesn't happen frequently, but Lockie already escaped death once. I want him to be safe."

"And you think he isn't." Jules brushed olive oil on the bread and put the slices on the grill.

"No, he is." I took a tomato out of the refrigerator. "I don't want my concern to add to his loss today."

"You are such a smart girl."

I didn't feel smart, I felt ineffective, unable to help him and guilty for the extra times I had lobbied for safety because it must have seemed like nagging.

"Call and invite Lockie to come up to the house for a nosh. Tell him I made his favorite cookies." Jules rubbed a piece of garlic across the bread and turned it over so it would be grilled on the other side.

"Cam's at the barn," I said crossing to the phone.

"Did he run into Greer?"

"They're out for a hack now."

"I think he's very good for her." Jules diced the tomato on a thick cutting board so quickly the knife blurred.

"Is she any good for him?"

"That's a mystery yet to be solved."

I keyed in Lockie's number and waited for him to answer.

"Hello."

"Hi. We're having a mid-afternoon snack. Would you like to come up to the house? Jules made your favorite cookies."

There was a pause long enough for me to think "Don't move backwards."

"I'll be there."

"See you."

I hung up and sighed with relief. "I hope Cam will stay for dinner."

***

My father was away as he so often was now and my grandparents were in New York holding down the Swope fort there, so we ate at the kitchen table.

10

Cap told us Mill was coming back from Argentina with Teche Chartier's polo ponies and would be home for weeks, absolutely weeks, before heading out for the spring season here. Europe was a question mark for Teche, still.

I was looking forward to seeing them together. Cap didn't make a big deal out of being separated from him for the last two months, but I knew they had to miss each other. We needed to have a welcome home party for Mill. Even if Teche would be throwing his own party, because he was a man who really enjoyed celebrations.

We were finishing dessert when Jules asked if we'd like to play cards. I shook my head.

"I'm calling it a day," Lockie replied and looked to me.

I nodded.

Everyone else must have felt like getting trounced by Greer so the cards were produced and they began.

Lockie and I drove to the carriage house and went inside. He turned on the lights while I waited.

There was a silence deep and profound. "Talia, are we in a relationship?"

"Yes."

"I mean a real one."

"Yes. What doesn't seem real about how we are together?"

Lockie was silent for so long I wondered if he had forgotten what we were discussing.

"I'm your first relationship, right? The first boy in your life."

"Yes."

"Do you know anything about me?"

"Everything important to know."

"Maybe." Lockie went to the kitchen and opened the refrigerator. "Do you want something to drink? Some of that coconut water you insist is so good for me?"

"It is good for you."

He tossed a container of it to me.

"You're not the first girl in my life."

I twisted the top of the juice box off and took a sip. "I'm glad you remember the others."

"I remember." Lockie walked back into the room. "Not all of them. There were quite a few."

"I'm sure there were."

That was the way the circuit was. I knew he had dated Jennifer Nicholson, although why he did had always eluded me since she seemed to be quite the bitch. I might have felt sorry she had broken her arm in multiple places in Florida, but I wasn't sorry she had gone home to Arizona.

"I liked Tink a lot. He was a strong and fearless rider with so much potential. He could see what a horse might become. We had a lot of fun together. I'm going to miss him."

"I'm sorry for your loss and his passing," I replied.

"I didn't always live wisely. My accident changed that but Tink's...death...Your father would have every right in the world to fire me. The only reason he hasn't is that you've been protecting me."

"My father hasn't fired you because he asked you to maintain certain parameters and you have. You are a decent and honest person."

"We're in a strange situation, Talia," Lockie said. "Up until now, I thought one of us would wake up. I thought it would be you."

"And I was supposed to do what exactly?"

"Find someone else, someone more appropriate."

"That's interesting because I never once thought any of these things that have apparently been on your mind for months."

"Think about what I had just been through and what it was like when I came to the farm. I had no future and no prospects. One of the daughters was the talk of the show circuit and the other had misbehaved with the last trainer."

"What? I was the talk of the show circuit? Why?" I couldn't think of anyone less worthy of gossip than me.

"Everyone said you had the disposition of a rank horse. You were sour, difficult and uncooperative. Does any of that sounds like an accurate description of you?"

I sighed.

"And they were right. On the first day you called me an idiot."

"Second day."

"First full day."

"Why did you stay? You could have gotten a gig conducting tours through the Grand Canyon."

"Talia. We're being serious. I considered it—not the Grand Canyon, but going back to California. Country Day School said they would always take me back."

"What stopped you?"

"You did."

"You like working with rank, sour horses?"

"Silly," Lockie protested.

"Everyone here has a past, everyone has made mistakes, everyone has experienced pain. The only thing that counts is what we do now."

"Are we going from being friends to being in a relationship?"

"If you need a definition, that's fine."

"It needs a definition because if we're friends, I can stay here alone and keep you away when I don't want you to get too close to me. If we're in a relationship, then I don't get to do that anymore."

"This isn't a decision I can make for you. I've already gone as far as I can toward you. You have to close the distance."

He paused. "I want to do that. Now can we go to bed? It feels like someone has taken a Saws-All to my head."

"Did you take your pills?" I asked, taking a step toward the kitchen to look for them.

Lockie put his arm around my shoulders and squeezed me tight. "That's why I stayed."

2

HE FELL ASLEEP almost immediately but I couldn't.

I had never asked Lockie or anyone else what his life might have been like on the show or event circuit prior to his accident. It was no secret how social that world was and I assumed he had a full life. That he was a heterosexual male well outnumbered by heterosexual females had to be like a kid in a candy shop. The same could also be said about Cam, but he was more open about appearing in public and being seen with a series of female friends, like the unfortunate photo of him with Sloane Radclyffe. I had never seen a similar photo of Lockie and a beautiful heiress.

It didn't matter to me what had happened before he arrived at Bittersweet Farm.

I sat up a little and watched him sleep.

The accident was something I wished had never happened but it brought him to us. He was safe and comfortable. He had a house. Wingspread had been returned to him.

So many things in life fall away. Lockie had a career of being an event rider and that fell away. He had changed living arrangements, apartments, farms and countries a half dozen times since he aged out. Those people and places were gone.

Not twenty-four hours earlier, his friend was killed in an accident very similar to his own. If Tinker Devlin's death made me question my life, and I didn't know him, what did it bring up for Lockie?

Plans are made and are never fulfilled, not for lack of trying but for unknowable reasons. What seemed like a straight road becomes a twisting, turning course that doubles back on itself and finally ends at an unpredicted destination.

I knew Lockie never thought he'd sink so low as to become the trainer/babysitter for two warring sisters in Connecticut. With a life-changing disappointment pressing down on him, Lockie never once complained, he never stopped smiling, he never spoke to us harshly, he was never rough with the horses.

How could I ever change my mind about him?

I reached over and kissed his cheek.

"Silly," he said.

"I'm sorry I woke you."

"I'm not."

***

Lockie was still asleep when I left the carriage house. In the pre-dawn, the lights in the barn seemed like a beacon and drew me steadily closer.

Cap had started to feed and I began to help.

"Is Lockie okay?" She dug a scoop into the grain.

"He's sleeping in, yesterday was difficult."

"No problem. We can leave his rides until this afternoon or split them between us. Cam can ride McStudly."

"They like each other. When is Mill getting here?"

"Around the middle of the month." Cap dumped the grain into a feed tub and moved down the aisle. "Why?"

"There's a show in Virginia and I was wondering if we should send a couple horses down. If Mill is here, I don't want you to go groom or ride Spare."

"Why can't Mill groom for me and I'll show and groom for Cam or Lockie?"

"That could work. Would you want to be on the road? Would Mill? It's your chance to be together."

Cap shrugged. "Here or in a White Line Motel, together is together."

"You're so easy-going," I said.

Cap laughed. "That is so untrue!"

Lockie did Bittersweet a great favor by asking Cap to come east to help us out and I wanted her to stay as long as possible. She was good with the horses and good with the Zuckerlumpens. Spare was on his best behavior for her. There was no downside.

"Are you happy in the apartment? Is there anything you need? Can it be improved?" I served CB his breakfast.

Cap dumped grain into Jetzt's tub. "It's fine. I'm not there very often. I eat up at the house and I'm here."

"Maybe you work too much. You should take a break. Go to a museum."

"The Old Newbury School dragged us to all the local museums. Maybe we could go to the pit where the colonials mined iron to make cannonballs. Wait, I've been there."

"If you want to take some time off let me know. When Mill comes, maybe."

"Trust me. He won't want to go anywhere that doesn't have to do with horses. The show is a good idea."

"Then we'll start to make plans."

Going south for a weekend would make it possible to show outside in better weather, at least it should be warmer. I didn't want to go as far as the Carolinas because that was a long haul. Virginia seemed about right. We could take the younger, less experienced horses and give them an introduction before the season started in earnest at home.

19

Wingspread, Citabria and Spare in the van. That made sense to me. There would be two in schooling jumpers and Cam could take Jetzt and McStudly in his trailer but that was beginning to sound like a caravan to me. Go down Friday afternoon, come back Sunday morning. It was doable. I would stay home. Very doable.

Cap and I finished feeding and were headed up to the house for breakfast when Pavel and Tomasz arrived to start on the stalls. My question of why Greer hadn't made it to the barn was answered when we went into the house. She was helping Jules with breakfast.

That made me happy. Greer didn't spend nearly enough time alone with Jules.

"Good morning," Jules said as Cap and I entered. "Where's Lockie?"

"If he's not here, he sleeping in." I went to the sink to wash up.

"I was worried about him last night," Greer said as she took a huge knife and, with a firm downward motion like wielding a sword, cracked a melon with it.

"He'll sleep the headache off and he'll be fine." I dried my hands.

I was trying to train myself not to worry about him every minute of every day. Once an hour should be plenty for anyone. The doctor had finally convinced me that Lockie was in no imminent danger. The headaches were not indicative of some impending catastrophe, rather something

20

that had to be managed for the rest of his life. When I accepted that, it was a relief but I still didn't want to see him, or anyone, in pain.

That was my Florence Nightingale mode as Greer termed it. She was as bad as I was but held it in better. If that wasn't true she wouldn't have called the police on the rider beating her horse behind the stabling area in Florida. Many people would have shrugged it off thinking that was the way some trainers were and getting involved was never a good idea.

I was so proud of Greer for turning in that horrid woman. We hadn't talked about it again but it probably made her feel as though she was evening her own score as well.

Just as we were sitting down, the door opened and Lockie entered.

"Were you going to let me starve?"

Greer served herself some scrambled eggs. "Yes."

Lockie hung up his jacket and went to his seat. "You could have called."

"I could have," I replied, "but I thought you needed to sleep."

"We were sure you'd make it up here by lunch," Jules added with a smile and passed him the basket of fresh rolls.

The door opened and Cam entered. "Are you eating without me?"

"We were trying to," Greer replied.

21

Cam went to the available chair next to her, hung his jacket on the back, and sat. "What are we having?"

"Homemade chicken sausage," Greer replied, spearing one and dropping it on his plate.

"Are there any peppers in there?" Cam asked. "I've had three months of seeing peppers in everything including dessert, I just want to give my stomach a rest."

"No peppers," Jules replied.

"There's a show in Aiken next weekend, can you get away to ride Tropizienne for me?" Cam asked.

Lockie looked at him in surprise. "Why can't you ride him?"

"Teche just bought Eschate and I'll be riding him in South Carolina."

"That big gray horse? Owned by Karsak?"

Cam nodded as he spooned a Matterhorn of scrambled eggs onto his plate.

"I don't want to seem rude but what do I and, by extension Bittersweet Farm, get out of it? Tropizienne's not our horse."

"Bring Counterpoint on the trailer."

"That's Greer's horse," Lockie said.

No one said anything.

"If you want to ride him, go ahead," Greer said. "I'm fine with Citabria and he's not ready for something as big as Aiken."

"Are you sure?" Lockie asked.

Greer nodded.

"There's a show in Northern Virginia in a couple weeks. Cap and I were talking about sending Jetzt, Spare and someone else. Just to start the season a little early and give them some mileage. You could ride Citabria there, Greer," I said.

"Sounds okay. And you'll stay home?"

"Someone has to hold down the fort," I replied.

"I guess you're planning on the van. Who's the third horse?" Lockie asked as he buttered his roll.

I thought about it. "Wing? McStudly's not ready for a public appearance."

There was silence for a long moment.

"We've got Tink's horse coming. I don't know how far along he is. If he's an event horse, he can jump."

"Have you ever seen him?"

"No," Lockie said. "Tink has...had great instincts for talented individuals."

"It would be a nice way to honor him," Greer said. "That's why he gave his horse to you, right? So you could give the horse a chance."

I was struggling not to cry as Jules rested her hand on my shoulder.

***

Lockie and Cam were working in the indoor and I was sitting on the edge of Greer's desk in her office.

"You're okay with Lockie continuing to ride Counterpoint?"

Greer looked up from her paperwork. "When it was all I thought I had, it was important. Now I have The Ambassador of Good Cheer and that is important. Not imaginary important."

This was not what I ever expected to hear from my sister. "You still want to show?"

"When I can get to it. I like Citabria very much but now that we're in a sensible training program, I can see there's no point in rushing him. So much of it is ego for some people. 'I'm so great, look at me. Please look at me.' It's pathetic."

That was something my sister never wanted to be seen as. Or vulnerable.

"Yes."

"I trust Lockie will buy, train and sell horses in the most responsible way. Bittersweet Farm will become known for our wonderfully talented horses and...I don't know what life holds."

"Do you object to Cam being here?"

"No, it's not a problem. I really like his mother, Kate. Even now, his grandfather has such a sharp wit. He tells colorful stories about being an actor, forgetting his lines, or having a set fall apart in the middle of a scene. It's a world I know nothing about, but Kerwin shares it with me. It

24

comes alive." Greer made a notation on a page. "We should have them over for dinner when Dad comes home."

"That sounds like fun." I thought for a moment. "I wonder if there's a part for him in Victoria's movie." I laughed.

"That movie will never be made," Greer replied. "Do you have any idea how many projects are bought and are never greenlighted? Hundreds every year."

"How can you be so sure? She's defied all the odds already."

I had to hand it to her. Victoria had actually concentrated long enough to write a book, somehow got it into shape to publish, and then we all saw it go to number one. She would do anything to see it on the big screen.

Greer must have gotten her bulldog nature from her mother. Of course, my father was no slouch in that department.

What had happened to me was anyone's guess. I had managed to inherit almost no ambition from my father. I didn't dream big dreams. I didn't want to be the center of attention. I just wanted to make life a little bit better for anyone I met, especially the horses. That was what I had inherited from my mother.

The door opened and Lockie paused there.

"Silly, will you get on Kyff? I have him tacked up for you."

"Sure," I said sliding off the desk. "I'll be right there."

Lockie disappeared down the aisle.

"What did he call you?"

I looked at Greer trying to remember what had been said. "Oh. Silly. Silly Filly."

In past times, Greer would have mocked me for that nickname. I would have never lived it down and would have regretted telling her.

Greer picked up her pen. "You're cute together."

"We'll hack out later?"

She nodded. "I have so much to catch up on but later in the afternoon will be good."

Kyff was waiting for me in the indoor. Lockie boosted me into the saddle and I settled in.

"What are we trying to find out?" I asked as I closed my legs on him.

"You're smart."

"True." I smiled back at him.

"I want to see how he is for you and then I'll get on and see how he goes for me."

"I'm not smart enough to know what that proves."

"How do you usually ride him? Contact-wise."

"I ride everyone on the buckle unless I'm working with you."

"He's never acted out with you?"

I thought. "I don't remember that he has."

"Just trot him like you normally would."

I urged Kyff forward and we trotted around the ring with loose reins.

"Walk. Do you remember what kind of bit they were using with him in Florida?"

Then I realized where we were going. "You think he was over-bitted."

"Yes. You get on and stay off his mouth and he's happy. I get on and ask more, sometimes he's good about it, sometimes he's not. He went nuts in Florida. Here he's no more nutty than the rest of us."

"You can't take him into the hunter ring and ride him on the buckle."

"No, but we'll use a softer bit on him. Jump off, we'll swap bits. It may take a while for him to realize he's not going to be smacked in the mouth every time someone takes up contact."

I patted his neck and slid off.

"Kyff's been in training for years and no one figured it out."

Lockie and I walked out of the ring.

"It's easier to assume the horse is misbehaving because he's a shit than to invest time in determining the reason why he's being a shit." Lockie smiled at me. "I think we just got a really good deal on a horse."

Ten minutes later, I was trotting around the ring with more contact than usual.

Lockie was at the center of the arena. "He's unsure but waiting to see what you're going to do to him."

I patted his neck, trotted for a few more strides then sat back and he walked.

"What's going on?"

"This makes me so angry."

"It should make you happy. I didn't want him. You did. You saw something in him and now he's happier. You should be very satisfied."

I turned Kyff toward Lockie and was about to speak.

"You can't save all of them."

I slid off, unfastened my helmet, and handed it to Lockie.

He put it on. "What kind of miniature head do you have?"

"It's small, not miniature, Mr. Big Head."

"That's Mr. Medium Head to you," Lockie said and adjusted the stirrup leathers. "Don't beat yourself up for what you can't do."

"Help us do the right thing by these guys, Lockie," I said.

He was about to stick his foot in the iron and instead put his arm around my waist and pulled me to him, kissing me like he meant it. Then he let me go and gave me a reassuring nod. "Yes, m'am."

3

THERE WAS NOTHING FOR DINNER when Greer and I got to the kitchen after our ride. Jules was nowhere to be seen, although her car was in the driveway.

There were footsteps, then Jules appeared wearing a pencil skirt and a silk blouse. "You're back. Get cleaned up, we're going out."

"I'll pass," Greer replied.

"Where are we supposed to be going?" I asked.

"Teche called and he invited us to his house."

"I don't want to go to a party," I said.

"It's not a party, it's dinner. Come on. We're meeting Lockie and Cam there."

After Lockie's ride on Kyff using the plastic mouth bit and seeing a noticeable improvement, he had gone to Acadiana Farm with Cam to discuss the possibility of riding at the Aiken show. It meant Lockie would fly to Tink's funeral and then fly to South Carolina without returning home.

It was a lot of traveling which was hard on him. I wasn't against it but I wasn't for the plan either. Lockie said that's what Tink would have done.

Maybe so, but I didn't want Lockie to start emulating Tink no matter how great a guy he had been. Pushing the boundaries was not only something I didn't approve of, it wasn't sanctioned by Dr. Jarosz.

"They're not coming home anyway," I said.

"That's right. I am also eating there and I would love for you to join the rest of us."

"We're taking our truck so we can leave whenever we want," Greer replied, picking up Joly and walking out of the kitchen.

Jules smiled. "You two are getting to be something of a team."

"I'm embarrassed to admit that Greer is everything Cam said she was. He could really see into the heart of her."

"She hates that she's so transparent to him. It makes her feel vulnerable when everything Greer does is to keep people at a distance," Jules replied. "But she'll get past that. Go put on something nice."

I went upstairs, showered and changed and Greer helped me with my hair, doing a nice French braid and a tight pinwheel roll, just like on a horse's tail.

"It looks cool," I said while studying it in the mirror.

"Wait. I have some picks." Greer rummaged through her desk drawer and held up little flowers set on pieces of fine wire.

She turned me around and wove those through the braid. "He'll be dazzled."

"I think we skipped that stage. The crushy does-he-like-me-I'll-wear-something-cute phase."

"That's what shouldn't go away."

I didn't understand.

"It's the I'm-dressing-for-you-because-you-are-the-most-important-person-in-the-world-to-me stage."

"Where did you learn that?"

"Victoria may be a lot of things, but she's not an idiot. Besides, I read the book. It's in there."

Cap went with Jules and I went with Greer in her lovely birthday present truck that she was just beginning to drive. After the incident in Florida, she didn't want to have anything to do with anything related to Cam but since she had been going to his mother's house and reading with his grandfather, Greer had relaxed about his presence in our lives.

Not only a wonderful rider and trainer, Cam was a steadfast friend. Lockie had come to rely on him and I wished Greer would allow herself to do the same because he was so good for her. Whether Cam thought Greer was good for him was another issue entirely.

Greer followed Jules down Teche's long driveway, arrived at the well-lit area in front of the house and parked next to Cam's truck. She shut off the engine and patted the steering wheel. "Let's go make the best of a bad situation."

"It's just dinner," I replied, getting out.

"We hope."

"Look at all these pretty girls!" Teche opened the door wide. "I think there's one for each of us."

I heard Greer sigh.

"Cappy?" A voice called out.

Cap bolted into the great room and into the arms of Mill.

"There's nothing I like better than a reunion," Teche said with a grin as he took our jackets and we all went inside.

The white polo shirt he wore proved Mill was even more tan than when he left for Argentina. Cap's smile couldn't have been any wider and she couldn't take her eyes away from him.

Teche brought around a tray of appetizers and I wished they had labels so I knew which to avoid. The shrimp with the head still on was obvious, but the other ones didn't look much safer. I pointed at one.

"That's a cheese grit tart," Teche replied with a grin. "Just a little bit of pepper in that one."

"No, thank you."

"You don't know what you're missing," he said.

"We have a pretty good idea," Greer replied.

Teche stopped in front of Jules with his offerings. "You should try the one in the upper right corner, I made it just for you."

I couldn't tell by the look of it what it could possibly be. There was a round crouton, a thin slice of something white, covered with something shiny and orange and topped by what seemed to be orange salmon roe.

Jules popped it into her mouth. "Delicious."

"Does it taste familiar?"

She thought for a moment. "You used my orange chili marmalade."

"And I'd like to talk to you about that," Teche said as he continued around the room. "Would you be willing to part with the recipe?"

"You hardly need me to tell you, if you run it through a spectrometer, you'll know exactly what I used."

"Caught me."

"So this isn't mine," Jules said.

"God, no, I finished that months ago. But it's your intellectual property and I wouldn't steal it from you. I'd buy it."

We all snapped our heads around to look at him.

"You want to buy a recipe I made one time and never wrote down?"

"I do! It's a hot addition to our prepared foods line-up. Say yes."

"No."

"What do you want?" Teche asked handing the tray to Cam who had no idea what to do with it.

"Anything I make while working for Andrew Swope belongs to him, and you know that."

"What does he want?" Teche replied. "This is between *bons amis*. We can make a deal."

Jules shook her head in disbelief.

"When are we having dinner?" Greer asked.

"Right now, if that's what you want," Teceh replied and led us into the dining room.

It was a beautiful house, decorated with fine antiques of the period but without the air of a museum. The oriental rugs were a bit worn, the chairs well-used, the table polished but not flawless.

He pulled out the chair at the foot of the table. "Miss Finzi, please do me the honor of sitting here so I have an unobstructed view of you throughout the meal."

I sat next to Lockie, Cap sat next to Mill and Greer sat across from Cam on the table's sides. Teche sat at the head.

"It's good to slow down and enjoy friends," he said as the food was brought from the kitchen. "That winter show circuit. One long party, wasn't it?" He looked at Cam.

Greer looked at Cam.

"I couldn't say since I was in the barn most of the time." Cam gave Greer a look.

Teche roared with laughter. "I like your style!"

34

As I focused on my salad, pushing the raw peppers to the side of my plate, Teche gave Jules the big pitch on why Chartier Spice was just the company to see her orange chili marmalade reach the pinnacle of the condiment category.

"But you don't have any other jams or jellies, do you?" Jules asked.

"There's nothing stopping you from inventing me something else," Teche replied reasonably.

"Nothing except that, as I said, I work for someone else."

"Quit."

My appetite instantly gone, I pushed the salad plate away from me.

"This is why we drove our truck here," Greer said and dropped her fork onto her plate for emphasis.

Jules smiled graciously. "I'm not sure what kind of offer that is, but thank you, I am already very happily employed. My father always said it was a mistake to discuss business over a meal, so let's finish this lovely dinner and leave business for another time."

Greer pushed back and stood. "I don't think..."

Cam stood. "I'll show you where the bathroom is." He went around to our side of the table and just about pushed her out of the room.

Part of me wished Cam hadn't interrupted her because I wanted to go home, too, and obviously he wasn't showing her where the powder room was because the front door opened and closed.

The main course was served and we had a choice of prime rib or mud bugs. It was no surprise to me that we all chose beef.

"This isn't business, so maybe we can talk about it. Lockie, what will persuade you to ride Tropizienne for me in South Carolina. Since Miss Jennifer is still on the mend, I'm down one rider and I got a new horse. Eschate. I paid a ton of spice for him but he's worth it!"

Did that mean there was a possibility that Jennifer would be coming back here? I had met too many people like her on the circuit to appreciate her attitude. She was highly competitive and not particularly concerned about her horse. Edge jockeys was the term I coined for people like her. Take big chances right at the edge for no reason other than the thrill. I was convinced it wasn't about the ribbons or the trophies or even the adulation they might receive. It was like sky diving and waiting until beyond the last best moment to pull the parachute cord, or racing a car at speed on the streets. What could they get away with?

The last time Jennifer tried it, she broke her arm in a headline stealing way in all the equestrian publications.

I thought we had seen the last of her but maybe she was healing faster than humanly possible.

"Let me get back to on that, Teche," Lockie said. "This is a bad week for me. I have a lot of traveling."

"That's easy to solve. You have my jet. What else is between you and saying yes?"

"I can recommend other riders to you," Lockie offered.

"They're not here in the neighborhood and I like the way you ride. I trust you and the horses do, too."

"I'll give you an answer in the morning." Lockie cut into his beef.

Cam and Greer entered, sat and no one mentioned their time away. I did wonder what he could say to her that would bring her back.

Dessert was happily free of peppers and after twenty minutes of recounting amusing stories regarding Florida, we all got ready to go. Except for Jules. She told Cap to take her car and Teche would give her a ride home later.

There was silence in Greer's truck on the trip, she left us off at the carriage house and went to the main house alone. I felt so bad for her and almost went back with the excuse that the horses needed to be checked. That wasn't true since Cap and Mill would be right there, but having her alone in a dark house seemed cold.

Lockie stopped me on the way out the door. "Give her some privacy. She's got Joly." He helped me take off my jacket.

"What does Cam say to her?"

"I have no idea."

"What would you say to her?"

"I have no idea."

"What would you say to me?"

"Let's go to bed. We have to talk about Aiken before the day is over."

We went upstairs.

"I don't want you to take on too much. I was concerned about how much traveling was involved, how much time you'd wait in airports, how stressful it would be. Since that's not an issue, it really is up to you."

"You're sure?"

"Yes. I just have one request."

Lockie pulled his shirt over his head. "What's that?"

"Please don't get any tattoos. My grandparents will freak."

He turned slowly and smiled. "Silly, you haven't seen me naked yet."

"Neither have they so let's just keep the status quo."

"Agreed." Lockie walked into the bathroom while I unbraided my hair.

4

"OKAY, EVERYONE SIT DOWN and be quiet for a few minutes. We need to have a talk," Jules said as we came in for breakfast.

"Doesn't talk imply an exchange of thoughts," Greer asked as she placed Joly's bowl on the floor.

"Fine. I'm having a brief monologue. Sit."

We did.

"I had a talk with your father last night after having a long discussion with Teche. Chartier Spices will be the proud recipient of my orange chili marmalade recipe. A lawyer will make the deal. There are two ways we—" Jules made a circle around us "—can be involved. We can take a buy-out or we can accept residuals. I mean royalties. I was starting to sound like my father." Jules shook her head.

"Which one will yield the greater profit?" Lockie asked.

"It's a gamble. Many new food products launched every year fail. Of course, most attempts are by small operations without Chartier's ability to get them onto shelves nationwide. This is not the first time someone suggested marketing something I created but with the odds being against success, I didn't bother."

"I think we should...are we allowed to speak now?"

"Yes, Greer," Jules replied.

"In the spirit of the Swope family, I think we should gamble on the profits that will accrue over time. It would be short-sighted to take a one-time pay-off."

She was so good with these concepts. "How much is the one-time deal?" I asked.

"That has yet to be negotiated."

"Can you ballpark it?" I asked.

"Substantial but not WOW, let's retire to an island off the coast of Italy."

"Does it matter?" I asked.

"Of course it matters," Lockie said.

I turned to him. "What does it have to do with us?"

Jules placed a cherry-walnut coffee cake on the table. "It matters. Andrew and I thought it would be equitable to divide the profits into thirds. One third going to the Swope Foundation, one third going to the charity of my choice and one third going to the upkeep of the farm and Greer's charity project."

"I don't think that's fair," I said. "Why should the farm get any money?"

"Because it will help you to take care of horses in need. Should there be money available in the future, Greer can use it to rehome horses or create a retirement community. I don't know the words for what is done, but Andrew and I have complete confidence that you will do it well and wisely."

We looked at each other.

"P.S. That was your grandmother's idea."

If this was a possibility for Jules, I was finding it difficult to understand why she didn't want to go off and invent some more food products. She could become a celebrity chef.

Jules nodded. "This was a one-off. As I've said time and again, I am very happy here. I don't need more, I don't need something else. Who wants eggs and who wants sausage?"

"Both," Lockie said.

The door opened and Cam entered. "Am I in time for breakfast?"

"Doesn't your mother feed you?" Greer asked.

"No, your grace," Cam bowed at the waist, and made a flourish with his arm, "she does not."

I braced for the explosion. If there was anything Greer hated, it was being reminded of her minor royalty lineage.

41

But there was no response and that was interesting in two ways. She didn't take offense and she had obviously confided in him.

I didn't know if I should ask her about this or not.

***

Lockie sat at the desk in the tack room, making out a list of everything that needed to be done in his absence. He was flying to Tink's funeral the next day, then going to South Carolina where he would show Tropizienne and Counterpoint for two days then fly home on Monday.

"What do you want me to do with Kyff?"

"If the weather is as good as the forecast suggests, hack him out. You probably won't have time but if you do, take him to the state park and go up the mountain. Go with Cap and take Spare."

"She'll want to stay here with Mill."

"He's going with the horses to Aiken so he's leaving today with Counterpoint."

"That doesn't seem very fair," I replied.

"He has a job."

"Everyone gets time off."

Lockie regarded me evenly. "He'll have time off when he gets back. When, since I've been here, have I had time off?"

I was shocked. "Do you want a vacation from the farm?"

"When have you had time off? This is your life. This is how you chose to live."

"When you get back we'll do something else."

He nodded. "Tink's horse is arriving this week. When he's sprung from quarantine, go pick him up. Come here."

I took a step closer and leaned over.

Lockie kissed me. "Why would I need a vacation from you?"

"I don't have a good answer for that."

"Yeah. See if you can help Greer. She's driving herself too hard. If you get Wing ready, we can spend some time with him."

The phone rang and he picked it up. "Bittersweet Farm."

I led Wingspread from his stall and put him on the aisle. His transformation from event horse to hunter prospect had been progressing well and I hoped Lockie would be able to begin showing him later in the spring. It was not that the farm needed one more horse to show but that Lockie needed to ride his own horse.

Lockie had invested two years in training him, but it was more than that. Wingspread was his event hopeful. CCI****, maybe. Everyone wanted to ride at Rolex Kentucky. Just competing was an accomplishment. Now that would never happen.

The choice was to sell Wing to someone else to event or repurpose him. Although Lockie had never said anything about it, I thought seeing his horse evented by someone else out of his own barn was probably going to keep reminding him of what he couldn't do any longer. Wingspread was Lockie's horse to ride but without the ability to become a show jumper, the only division left was hunter and he could find some success there.

With Tink's horse arriving at the farm any day, we were going to have essentially the same choices with him. Nassau could be evented by someone, Freddi perhaps, or maybe he had the talent to make it as a show jumper. Either way, the gelding had to do something with his life.

CB, with only his swish going for him, was becoming the least complicated issue on the property.

I put my saddle on Wing, tightened the girth, and led him to the mounting block. We were trotting around the indoor when Lockie arrived.

"You don't do anything," he said after watching us for a few minutes.

"Give me a hint on how I'm supposed to take that," I replied, pulling back to a walk.

"Horses like you because it's as though you're not there."

"Can I buy another clue?"

"Most riders are active—"

"This is sounding worse and worse," I replied.

"It shouldn't. This is a real talent. When I get on, I'm doing something. I have expectations. You get on and have no expectations. They'll have a cookie when it's over no matter what. You're not trying to engage their hind quarters, drop onto the bit, lengthen, shorten, speed up or down."

"And?"

"Because of that, they all relax with you."

I pulled up next to him. "Do you?"

"Yes."

"I don't drive you crazy?"

He put his hand on my knee. "Of course not. Do you worry about that?"

"Yes."

"Don't." Lockie smiled. "You could give me an oatmeal cookie once in a while, then pat me on the butt and tell me what a good boy I am."

I slid off Wing, dug into my pocket for what was left of a cookie and handed him the pieces. "You're the best boy." I patted his butt. "Don't go to Aiken."

"You say the same thing every time I have to leave."

"And I mean it." I removed my helmet and leaned my forehead against his. "Get on your horse and tell me what to do with him while you're gone."

Lockie took my helmet and made a big show of how difficult it was to fit on his head, then he mounted easily.

"Do you love that horse," I asked as he adjusted the stirrup length.

"Love's a big word and I don't know that I should use it for an animal. I like and respect him. Do I feel the same

45

about Wing as I do about you? No, not in the least." He held Wing back for a moment. "Do you feel the same about CB as you do about me?"

"No."

Those were two different kinds of love.

***

My grandparents came up from the city that afternoon, ostensibly to have dinner, but, in reality, to talk about the orange chili marmalade conundrum since my father was in Colorado. I hugged my grandmother almost hard enough to leave bruises, but needed to express how grateful I was that she had suggested we might set up a project to rehome horses. All my thoughts began and ended with the Ambassador of Good Cheer and it hadn't occurred to me so quickly that we might go in another direction as well.

It was a relief to have them with us and dinner was a spirited event as all sides of the issue were discussed, even those I didn't realize existed. We all avoided assuming how much this deal was worth, but suspected Teche would be more than fair since he treated Cam and Lockie with generosity.

As soon as dessert was finished and there was nothing but crumbs left, Lockie and I left for the carriage house to pack for his trip. He needed one suitcase for his clothing for the funeral and another that could be sent with Cam containing his riding gear.

Sitting on the edge of the bed after we were finished, Lockie looked exhausted. I didn't know what to say to him. Funerals were always about ragged and raw emotions, a time for people to accept their loss, even if they hadn't worked through it yet. The people not unglued by the situation, wound up trying to comfort the ones who had. There was really nothing that could be said or done but simply to live through it.

Lockie patted the bed next to him and I sat.

"Tell me about Tinker," I said. "Tell me about the first time you saw him ride. Tell me about the most fun you had together. Tell me why you will miss him."

He said nothing for a long moment then began to answer my questions.

***

Early the next morning, Lockie left for the airport. Cap and I put shipping boots on Counterpoint for his ride then Mill and I drove him to Acadiana Farm. Mill stayed, I came home alone. Tracy was scheduled to catch up with them in Aiken.

Greer met me in the barn.

"Please. No bad news."

"No. Let's all go to the Inn for lunch. We'll wear our barn clothes and give the fancy people something to talk about."

I shrugged as we went to the tack room. "Greer. I don't want to be nosy and if you don't want to tell me, that's fine, but when Cam didn't show you the bathroom, where did you go?"

"We took a walk to the barn. He told me about the horses."

"That's it?"

"Not very exciting."

I was sure there were parts she was leaving out. How did he persuade her to go to the barn and not the truck?

"Okay," I replied.

"You seem a little confused about it."

"To be completely honest, yes. You were upset when you got up from the table and then you two just strolled to the barn?"

"I'll try to explain it. You're riding down the road. There's a plastic grocery bag caught on a tree branch and it's flapping in the breeze. What do you do?"

"Turn the horse's head."

"There you go."

If that was it, kudos to them both. Cam figured Greer out. Greer knew what he was doing and didn't fight it. Small steps.

"Do you want to ride now?"

"Sorry, I have to work. There's a project—"

"Besides Good Cheer?"

"Yes."

I followed her out of the main barn. "Are you taking too much on?"

"I don't think so. Finally I'm good at something."

"Not finally," I objected.

"It feels like that."

"None of us here cares about the heights you can reach...just be nice. That's what is important. Do good."

Greer smiled. "That's what I'm doing. You'll see. I still have work to do before lunch but we'll ride later, okay?"

"I'd love that," I replied. "Hug?"

We put our arms around each other and gave a quick squeeze.

"Don't expect me to be a replacement for your boyfriend," Greer said, dropping her arms and walking away.

"I wouldn't make that mistake since he's a lot bigger than you are," I called after her.

She shook her head.

I turned to find Cap getting ready to ride Spare.

"We'll give him about twenty minutes, you can take him down the road, and then we'll get ready for lunch. We're all going out. Don't change though, we're supposed to look like farmers. That will shock people."

"Really? It used to shock people if you wore a see-though top but now it's if you wear overalls."

"I think we're supposed to wear boots and breeches.

Cap tightened Spare's girth. "Whose idea is this?"

"Greer."

"What's she rebelling against?"

"You don't need GPS coordinates to hit the nail on the head, do you?"

"You make me sound smarter than I am," Cap said as she unclipped Spare from the cross-ties. "It must be her other family."

If the Kensington-Rowes were my family, I'd rebel, too. The truth was that it was amazing Greer turned out to be the decent person she was. She had gone through high school like an armored vehicle, she could wield words as weapons and she knew where to attack so she could inflict the most pain. Only because it had been done to her.

Once the pressure of accomplishment had been removed, and she accepted the fact that we wanted her in our family, Greer began to shine. The success of the Ambassador of Good Cheer was hers alone. We all recognized it.

Victoria didn't. If Greer had become engaged to a scion from an old money family, that would have been an accomplishment. Setting up a charity was all too pedestrian, too Swope-ish. The Kensington-Rowes were supposed to float above such common activities.

That Victoria had written a book jam-packed with scenes circus contortionists would have difficulty reproducing and having it go to number one was laudable, while popcorn balls in the shape of a dog's head was laughable.

If it would make Greer happy for us to have lunch at the Inn looking like we had just left the barn, which would be accurate, then I was good with that. There was no one I had to impress.

"It is her other family," I replied.

"There is no way I could live down to the standards my father set," Cap replied and led Spare out of the barn.

Since he had left detailed notes, I knew what Lockie wanted me to focus on while he was away. Spare was still young enough that changes could surprise him, then he tended to get a bit strong. Our goal was to prove to him that everything was boring and routine, that having a jump in front of him shouldn't be cause for alarm or excitement.

We had set up a simple gymnastic with poles on the ground to trot over in a relaxed manner. Going between standards was not a cue to rush. After about fifteen minutes, going in, around and over the poles, I put the rail on the standards up to about two feet. Spare over-jumped it. I appreciated his enthusiasm or his desire not to hit a rail but this was excessive.

Cap trotted him in large circles until he calmed down, then we tried the gymnastic again. He rushed and stepped on a rail. She went back to trotting the circles.

"Is it me?" she asked.

"No, he's just full of himself. If he's sharp here, what happens when he enters the stadium and there's an enormous Jumbotron to one side?"

"Or a Jack Russell runs across the ring."

"Exactly," I said. "He can't be emotional. This is his job and he needs to be able to focus. Try it again."

Cap turned Spare for the combination and there was a definite improvement as he adjusted his pace on his own.

That's what we wanted to see. Spare should learn to figure these things out for himself. "One more time."

She trotted a large circle and incorporated the small jump in it. Spare took it calmly.

"Again."

Cap continued around and the result was the same.

"Good boy! That's enough for today. Take a little walk, put him away and we'll go to lunch."

I spent the next half hour pulling manes, tidying them, maintaining a good length to braid without being too thick. Call and Whiskey had their whiskers trimmed. Jetzt looked so sleek, I suspected Greer had spent some time grooming him when CB and I had taken a walk to the stream.

5

"HAVE YOU HEARD from Lockie yet?" Jules asked as we sat around the table at the Inn.

Some patrons had glanced toward us as we entered but I couldn't be sure if it was just because four young women were walking through the dining room, or because of our breeches and half chaps. In a tailored navy blue suit, Jules was dressed appropriately for lunch at a country inn, so I assumed they were really focusing on her.

"No," I replied and opened the menu.

"I heard from Cam," Greer said.

I looked up.

"He went to the funeral with Lockie. Then they flew to South Carolina."

"Did he know Tinker Devlin?" I asked.

"No."

"That was very nice of him," Jules replied.

"Has anyone heard from Mill?" Cap asked with a smile.

"Yes." Greer closed her menu. "Cam said Mill performed routine first aid on Red Savina somewhere in North Carolina but everyone is fine."

"Lovely. Everyone heard from everyone so we're all happy," Jules said.

"Darling! What are you doing here?"

"You spoke too soon," Greer said as Victoria hurried over to the table.

Victoria trained her gaze on each of us in turn. "Don't you all look...countrified."

"Go away. Pretend you don't know me and I'll do the same," Greer said.

Victoria leaned over to air-kiss her. "I must catch you up on all the news."

"We'll survive without it." Greer waved at a waitress.

Victoria, dressed in red, pulled a chair away from another table. "You don't need this, do you?" she asked the startled patrons.

The waitress arrived at the table. "Will we be four or five?"

"I don't want to interrupt but if you insist," Victoria said.

We were so far from insisting.

"Five," Jules said.

"What would you ladies like for lunch?"

"A Lucrezia Borgia poison ring," Greer replied, handing the menu to the waitress.

"That's such a clever quip," Victoria patted Greer's hand. May I use it in my next book?"

"Sure. If you show us how to perform the act at location 1286."

Victoria laughed. "Just because I wrote it, doesn't mean I have personal experience with each and every scene."

I looked at Cap and she was rolling her eyes in disbelief.

"The movie is going forward, in the way Hollywood does these deals. Oh, that reminds me." Victoria removed the checkbook from her bag and wrote out a check, then handed it to Greer. "Give this to your father, please."

Greer looked at it. "What's this?"

"Andrew so kindly helped me out when I was...low on cash. This should cover the shop and the condo."

"Is it going to bounce?" Greer asked.

"I should say not. That's only part of the money I've gotten from the book and the movie deal."

All I could think was "Can we go home now?"

"Been there, done that," Cap said to me in a whisper. "Luckily no one is playing you, Greer," she said in a normal tone of voice.

"It looks like dishy Adam Saunders is going to play Cam, I mean Gillette MacDonnell and Titania Guilford will play Aria."

"With her, it's definitely typecasting," Greer replied.

I never heard of the actress, but, obviously, Greer had and didn't hold a positive opinion of her.

"She'll sleep with him, of course."

"Of course," Victoria replied. "Do you mean in real life?"

Greer glared at her mother. "Did you stop reading *Hello! Magazine*? They can't keep up with her since she changes her partners more often than her panties."

Jules pressed her fingers to her mouth to keep from laughing.

"I don't read trash like *Hello!*"

"Unless you're in it."

"They did such a nice article on the family several years ago," Victoria explained to us.

"I'm sure the Kensington-Rowes deserved it," I said.

"We're an important family," Victoria said. "We have direct lineage to the Domesday Book. We can trace ourselves back over twelve hundred years. We are original Anglo-Saxons."

"None of that trashy Norman blood for us," Greer said over her.

Victoria continued. "Andrew can trace himself back about one hundred and fifty years."

"If he wasn't good enough for you, you shouldn't have married him," Greer said.

We waited.

"Andrew is a very dear man. I was quite taken by him."

"And his bank account," Greer replied.

"It's as easy to fall in love with a rich man as a poor man, darling, you'll learn that some day."

"What page is it on? I seem to have missed it in *Tight and Loose*."

"It's in the next book." Victoria smiled.

I pushed back from the table. "Excuse me, while I visit the Ladies Room."

I walked through the dining room and out the front door, keying in a phone number as I went. By the time I reached the sidewalk, the phone was answered.

"Talia?"

"Dad, is it at all possible for you to come home? Greer will need to see you."

***

Late that night, I heard his footsteps in the hall outside my bedroom. There was a knock on her door.

"Greer, may I come in?"

"Yes."

I heard her crying for what seemed to be a long time, then she stopped.

It was impossible for me to understand how someone like Victoria could have given birth to someone as remarkable as Greer. I hoped Victoria would move to Los

Angeles and associate with people who were undoubtedly more like her and let her daughter get on with her significant contributions to the world.

Just as I was about to turn off the light, my phone rang.

"Hi. You're missing all the excitement here," I said.

"You're missing the excitement here. There was a horse with a hock the size of an orange."

"Teche's horse?"

"No," Lockie said, "but the owner, trainer and rider were either out to dinner or not in Aiken yet, leaving a very inexperienced groom in charge, so we helped her out."

"Will the horse be okay?"

"Yes. The vet came and the trainer finally arrived. A little drunk, I think. It's always a good policy not to drink and ride."

"Good advice. Did you ever?"

"I might have done some things I shouldn't have but they never involved horses," Lockie replied. "Unless you want to point out the times I gave a certain Herr Geist a bottle or two of brew."

"When are you going to show him?"

"There's a dressage competition in New Jersey later on in the spring," Lockie said.

"What's the reluctance?"

"You're doing so well on him, I keep hoping that *losgelassenheit* will be confirmed."

"What's that?"

Lockie paused. "It's a little bit hard to translate. Happy camper."

"No."

"No, but that's the idea of it. You want the horse to be calm but also willing. When you ride CB, he's very happy. He'd do anything for you. When I ride him, he does what I ask but he's ticked off. I'd like to have his good disposition permanent for both of us."

"Does the drinking and riding thing apply to him, too?"

Lockie laughed. "It's worth a try. I don't think they drug test for alcohol."

"Does that mean we have to bring a keg to every show?"

"What a reputation we'd get. There's another option, Tal. He's your pet pony. Your insanely over-qualified pet, but there's no requirement for him to do anything but carry you through the woods. You can choose that."

This was an issue I had considered more than a little in the past months.

Life had been good to Lockie but still he had lost the direction he had been going in. He never complained but he had spent nearly two years in Germany working with a top dressage trainer. If he could ride jumpers and have a dressage horse then only one element of his dream—cross country—would be missing. That wasn't such bad compensation.

"I work. You work. Greer works. CB can do a little something, too. If you want a dressage horse, and would enjoy competing again, use him."

Lockie didn't reply for a moment. "Tal..."

I didn't want him to thank me. "It's good publicity for the barn."

"Unless he enters the arena and does an interpretive dance instead of the dressage test. What did you do with the sugar lumps today?"

"I gave them an option of riding without stirrups for the entire lesson."

"And they complained."

"So they rode in two-point the whole time. Their legs were shaking when they got off."

Lockie laughed.

"I miss you," I said.

"I haven't been gone long enough for you to miss me."

I didn't reply.

"I miss you, too. Cam won't put flowers in my hair. I asked but he said he's not that kind of guy."

"Who would have guessed," I said.

"Talk to you tomorrow. Turn off the light and go to sleep, Talia."

"Goodnight, Lockie."

The farm was not the same without him.

***

Entering the house after doing the morning chores, I found my father standing by the counter, wearing blue jeans and a polo shirt, holding a mug of coffee. "Good morning, Talia."

I crossed the room and put my arms around him. "Thank you."

"Thank you for calling me."

As I cleaned up at the sink, Greer entered followed by Joly and they went directly outside.

"Greer gave me the check from Victoria," he said.

"Does it cover what she's cost since she arrived?"

"Financially, yes. What she's cost otherwise, no." He went to his place at the head of the table and sat.

Jules brought a large platter of sausages and home fries to the table. Greer came in with Joly, fed him, cleaned up and sat down.

"Before we start eating, I want to say something to the family. This is an election year and I have a very full schedule."

I nodded.

"My father has agreed to take on a greater portion of running Swope and I will do more from home. I'm sorry I wasn't present in your lives the way I should have been but..."

Greer had her head down and my father reached across the table to pat her hand.

"We'll all do better," he finished. "Now. What's our schedule for today?"

I looked up in confusion. How did it become our schedule? "Excuse me?"

"I know I won't be much help but I'll give it a shot."

"Greer and I were going to Newburgh to pick up a horse this morning, but I don't have to go," I said.

"What's in Newburgh?" he asked.

"International quarantine. Lockie's friend left him his horse and he's free to leave today," Greer said.

"That's fine, you go, Dad. Greer can easily handle the horse by herself. We're short-handed without Lockie so Cap and I have plenty to do."

That was true. Once the Acadiana horses returned from Florida, our temporary help stayed at their own barn and Tracy had taken some time off after being away for almost three months. When we all agreed to that, it seemed that the beginning of March would be quiet but that proved not to be the case. Any difficulties would only last for a few days because Lockie and Cam would be back on Monday.

"Is that okay with you Greer?" he asked.

"I'd like that. You can hold Joly."

At the sound of his name, Joly finished his search for a missed molecule of his breakfast and came to sit next to Greer.

Cap entered. "Sorry I'm late. Is there anything left?"

"We just started," Jules replied. "Without our young men in attendance, there is always plenty. I'll have to revert to restaurant quantities with them here this year."

"We'll have to eat in the dining room," my father said.

That's where the large table was. I could picture it—Cam, Mill, Lockie, Cap, my grandparents, my father, Jules and the two of us. What an extended family we would make.

"We should plan a big 4th of July party," Jules said as she helped herself to some home fries. "Not just to have a party but to celebrate what the day means."

"That would be wonderful."

"I wonder if Cam's father would be able to read The Declaration of Independence. He has such a beautiful voice," Greer said. "He's not strong enough now but in four months he could be."

"Excellent idea," Jules said. "Maybe Cam could help him."

"Maybe Cam could dress up as a Revolutionary War soldier," I said.

"Maybe we could have some reenactors in. They could use the front field," Greer replied.

Cap looked up from her plate. "Women in long dresses making soap or something?"

"Something."

"What about the local museum. Could someone tell us how cannonballs were made from the iron ore mined locally?" I asked. "Someone else talk about the farming of the day."

"You know who has those Belgian Draft horses," Cap said snapping her fingers.

"Daisy and Rufus," I supplied.

"Who's the owner?" Cap asked.

I couldn't remember.

"Mr. Auerback," Greer said.

"That's right. He'd bring them here with his wagon. He shows them off at the county fair every year."

Greer pushed back from the table. "I have to go make some notes."

"You have to go to New York," I reminded her.

She stopped. "Oh."

"Twenty minutes one way or the other won't make a difference, will it?" my father asked.

"We're supposed to be there at noon, but no, I don't think they'll have our heads if we're a little late," Greer said then hurried out of the room.

"She'll have it organized by tomorrow," I said, finishing my tea.

"She's just like her grandmother," my father replied with a touch of pride. "My mother must have lead armies in a previous life."

~ 6 ~

CAP AND I spent the morning exercising horses, turning some out and bringing others in. When Butch came in, he seemed sore, so went on the list for Dr. Fortier to check over the following day. The vet was already making the trip for Tink's horse, so it was always better to do everything at the same time. Now that Cam was home, I wanted a review of Whiskey's status to determine if he was sound enough to be returned to a fitness program.

The Zuckerlumpens were due after school. I planned to give them a lesson for a half hour, then Cap would hack out with them. It was not for a stroll. They would be trotting up and down the hills for endurance. While Poppy was somewhat farther along than Gincy, neither of them were as tight in the saddle as I would like to see. They both retained bad habits from their previous trainers and if I didn't keep after them, the girls defaulted back to the old way. With the progress they were making, I wanted to keep them going in the right direction until they didn't revert when I wasn't watching.

Cap and I went to the house for lunch. It seemed, because it was true, there were fewer of us than ever. Jules made soup and we had pressed sandwiches of grilled eggplant, sliced tomatoes, mozzarella, fresh basil leaves and olive oil. They were so delicious I almost thought that Jules was trying to cheer us up because everyone was away, but her food was always fantastic. Dessert was supposed to cheer us up and she brought a delicate pistachio cake with swirls of nougat frosting covered with chopped, toasted nuts to the table. It worked. I was well cheered.

Late in the afternoon, when the Zuckerlumpens were gone, Lockie's truck and trailer came slowly down the driveway. Greer stopped at the door and I went out to greet them.

"You should have been home by three. What took so long?" I asked.

"Vhere are your papers?!" Greer said with a German accent as she went around the back of the trailer. "You'll be surprised."

My father nodded.

Greer got into the trailer, unhooked him and I released the tail bar.

The liver chestnut backed slowly down the ramp. Not only was he huge, he was gorgeous. With a crested neck, two white socks, and a strip down his face, he appeared to be even larger than CB.

"What breed is he?" Cap asked.

"Holsteiner," Greer replied. "Like Citabria."

"Poor thing," I said. "Traveled so far, was in prison and now he's arrived someplace where he knows no one."

I held out an oatmeal cookie to him. He had no idea what to do with it.

"Maybe he's not hungry," my father said. "I am. I'll meet everyone up at the house."

"Sure," I replied.

"We'll hand-walk him for a while," Greer said. "Why don't you call Lockie and see if there's anything special we should do."

I went into the barn and stopped by CB's stall. "You would not believe the horse who just made the flight from Germany. Maybe you would." I offered him the cookie and he knew exactly what to do with it.

Lockie answered the phone. "Hi, Tal. Did Tink's horse get there?"

"You bet. Is there anything you want us to do with him?"

"Is there something wrong with him?"

"Cap's hand-walking him now. He seems fine. He's huge, Lockie."

69

"Are you saying he's bigger than CB?"

"Yes, I think he's heavier. Bone and weight."

"Did he drag someone off the trailer and through the yard?"

"No, he seems sweet but deprived."

"In what way?"

"He doesn't know what an oatmeal cookie is."

I heard voices in the background.

"I'm sure you'll teach him. I have to go. If you have any problems, call me back. I'll call you when my day is over."

"Okay."

We said goodbye.

I missed him and felt uneasy. I kept checking to see if I had forgotten to do something with all the activity. Everything was in place but I wondered if I could have missed whatever it was that was trying to get my attention.

As Cap finished walking the gelding, I went to the lower barn and made sure everything was closed, especially Beau's stall. He was trying to learn how to unlatch his door and I had already put a clip on it to prevent him from succeeding.

We checked the gelding over thoroughly, took his temperature, felt his legs and he was one hundred percent fine.

Cap pulled a blanket over him. "What's wrong?"

"It's a feeling. I didn't do something that I was supposed to. I didn't notice something I should have. I don't know what it is."

"When did it start?" Cap put the horse into the stall next to Kyff.

I shook my head.

"I've been with you for the last two hours. If you missed something, I would have caught it."

We closed the door and got in my truck.

"I know that. I appreciate how responsible you are."

I headed the truck toward the house.

"Maybe it's not the horses," Cap said.

"Then what?"

"Lockie is riding jumpers tomorrow. You do..."

"Worry?" I supplied.

"You're concerned. I understand."

"Did I pack everything he needs?"

"Didn't he check?"

"Yes. It's not like he's in Outer Mongolia. Whatever he needs, he could get there. All the tack went down with Mill and the horses."

"So are you worrying about his underwear?" Cap asked.

She made me smile. "He would ride without it, couldn't he?"

"I wouldn't want to see that," Cap admitted.

I parked near the house.

"Listen, Tal," Cap said as we were getting out. "When I met Mill I was borderline hysterical. Everything that could go wrong in my life was heading straight down and picking up speed. When you're checking the burners on the stove

71

every time you go by, or checking the stall doors, or the water, or whatever it is, you should wonder if it's really about that or it's about something else."

"Like what?"

"I felt like my life was out of control and I was right in the sense that I couldn't do anything about what was going on around me. My father was happily parading around, touting his bigamy as a badge of honor. I had moved three thousand miles from home and didn't see how I would ever get back. I had to work in my mother's restaurant when all I ever wanted was to be outside with the horses. Couldn't change any of it and didn't."

We paused at the kitchen door.

"We worry about the things we can't control and don't pay attention to the things we can. At least, that's the way it seems to me." Cap walked into the house.

Everyone was at the table, prepared for dinner.

"You can start without me. I'm going to get cleaned up."

"Okay," Jules replied as she stood by the stove.

In my bedroom, I pulled off my breeches and pulled on some sweats then sat at my desk. I opened the lowest drawer, took out a book that had belonged to my mother and put my hand on it.

"Are you coming down to dinner?" Greer asked from the doorway and Joly trotted over to see me.

I nodded.

"I could use some help tomorrow because Amanda's going to be away for a few days. If you could make some calls for the Fourth of July event, that would be good. I'd like to get commitments from people before much longer. Some are probably booked a year in advance. We'll need to determine who we can't get and find someone to replace them."

"Dad's good with this?"

"Yes, we discussed it in detail. That's pretty much all we could do while waiting for the paperwork to be sorted out." Greer started to leave. "He seems like a nice horse."

"Get on him tomorrow and we'll see."

Greer laughed. "If he bucks himself inside out, you want me to wind up in the dirt and not you."

"Am I that transparent?"

***

Cap and I had just made the last pass of the barns, checking on Tink's horse, who was fine and didn't want a carrot either, when tack room phone rang.

"Bittersweet Farm," I said.

"Hi, this is Eveleigh Nysell from Flying Y Films. Is Lockie Malone available?"

"No, I'm sorry he's not. Is there anything I can do for you?" I asked.

Please say no, I thought.

"I'd like to visit the farm tomorrow," she said.

"Why?" I asked and motioned Cap to come to the tack room.

"I have to scout locations for a film we may be doing."

It was too late in the conversation to say I didn't speak English but I did the best I could. "I'm not the barn manager, Lockie Malone is, and this is something you would have to discuss with him."

"Do you have a contact number for him?"

I put the mouthpiece of the phone against my leg. "This is Victoria blowback. Some movie company wants to come here to scout locations."

"Tell them no."

I had already dug myself a little bit of a hole but I could fill it in fast. "I'm sorry, he's out of town and won't be back until next week."

"He doesn't have a phone where he is?"

"He went on a retreat. No phones allowed."

"Studying to be a Buddhist monk," Cap whispered to me.

"I'll call the main office and they can go get him."

"It's a Buddhist sanctuary. No talking allowed."

She was annoyed with me. "My boss isn't going to be happy."

"I'm sorry we couldn't please your boss but there are a couple hundred farms within the Tri-State area. I'm sure you can find one who will be able to say yes."

She hung up on me.

I held out the phone to Cap to hear from herself that the connection had been broken.

"I've been through it. You don't want anything to do with these people."

"Very true," I replied. "Do you think this is what I was feeling?"

"You're psychic now?" Cap asked as she started up the stairs to her apartment.

"I do have some mindreading skills. I know when CB wants a cookie."

Cap laughed. "That would be always."

"Have a good night," I said and waited for her door to open then turned off the lights. "CB. I have a cookie for you."

***

My father was in his room, Greer was in her room and Jules was in the den watching an old movie.

"Hey, come sit next to me," she said and patted the couch.

75

I plunked myself close enough to be touching. "I got a call from a movie company and they want to scout us for a location."

"For Victoria's movie?"

"Has to be."

"She probably suggested the farm."

"I told the woman that Lockie was the one to ask and he's on a Buddhist retreat. Since speaking is not permitted, she can't talk to him. I guess technically if they had a phone, which they don't, she could talk to him but he couldn't answer."

Jules laughed.

"There's no way I'm letting her distracted him with this nonsense when he's showing over huge fences."

She put her arm around me. "He'll be fine."

I nodded.

"This is the first version of *Captain Blood*. Peter Blood is a doctor who is convicted of treason and is sent to be a slave in the West Indies."

"Another one of your happy movies," I said.

"It's an adventure and a romance," Jules replied. "He escapes and becomes a pirate."

"That makes it a little more believable."

"You'll see." Jules gave me a squeeze and we settled in to watch the pirates duel beneath the palm trees.

Captain Blood got the girl in the end, so Jules was right and it was a romance. Even if they couldn't be heard.

I kissed her goodnight and went upstairs to get ready for bed. Lockie called just as I finished my shower.

"Is everything all right there," I asked.

"Yes, why?"

"I had a feeling earlier but then we got a call from a location scout for Victoria's movie."

"They're going forward?"

"Seems like it."

"How's the horse?"

"Fine. He's eating and drinking water. I put him next to Kyff."

"Are you able to show McStudly?"

"Do you have someone interested in him?"

"Yes. Cam and I ran into Egan Wade of Gone To Ground Farm this morning and one of his trainers will drive up from New Jersey to have a look."

"We haven't done that much with him," I said.

"No, but he's got plenty of potential. That's what they're buying."

McStudly had been expected to stay in training until the end of the year, so this was a change in plans. "Okay."

"It's the right thing. Egan will take his time with McStudly. He'll be well cared for and given as much attention as he gets here."

I didn't say anything.

"We rescued him from the track. That was a very positive change in his life. Be happy for him, wish him well, and send a bag of cookies with him."

I knew Lockie was right. When someone was paying as much as McStudly cost, the owners would be protective of their investment. He would live in a lovely barn where grooms would pet him just like here.

"When are you coming home," I asked.

"Miss me?"

"Not at all," I replied.

"Yeah, I feel the same," Lockie said. "Have a good night."

"You, too."

He hung up.

I looked at the phone. It rang and I clicked it back on.

"You don't miss me at all?"

"Be serious. I miss you when you go to the feed store."

"I thought someone had to at least leave town."

"Have you ever missed anyone?" I asked.

"Not until now," Lockie replied.

⚛ 7 ⚛

IT WAS DRIZZLING when I woke. I pushed back the covers and went into Greer's room.

"Can I get in with you two?"

"If you can get Joly moved over," she said.

Joly was repositioned to the opposite side and I got into the bed.

"Lockie called last night and he thinks they have a buyer for McStudly. Egan Wade from Gone To Ground Farm."

"That's a top barn and Wade's very good. I think he was on the junior Olympic team. How lucky for McStudly."

"One of the trainers is going to come up and look at him today so will you ride him and I'll try to be a good saleswoman?"

"He's big and bright and has a great future ahead of him. You don't have to say more than that. And I'll ride him if you help me."

"Sure."

"Go through the list of shows for the spring and choose two or three a month. One or two that would be good for the ponies. One that would be good for hunter division and one that would be good for jumper. We'll need to start sending in our entries."

"Do you want to go to Devon?" I asked.

We had ridden in the Devon Horse Show and County Fair every year except last year. Rui couldn't get our acts together. He said it wasn't an important show anyway.

Devon, over one hundred years old, was definitely one of the most important shows on the Eastern Seaboard. It was quite probably my favorite show because of its history and setting. There were carriage classes, sidesaddle and Shetland pony races in addition to every conceivable hunter, jumper and family classes. It was a fun show to attend because with everything going on, I was able to forget about the competition.

Our ponies weren't ready for Devon but if Whiskey stayed sound, he should go. Wingspread could go First Year Green Hunter. Greer could ride Counterpoint. That would fill the van.

"I've been thinking about it. I'm so busy."

"What have you done with my sister?" I asked and was nudged in response.

"I know. I never turned down a chance to show before but we'd be away nearly a week."

"A long weekend, if you arranged it well."

"Lockie could show Counterpoint. I could never do as well as he does on him anyway."

"Don't say those kinds of things. You're starting out. When Lockie was starting out do you imagine he was as good as he is now?"

Greer thought for a moment. "Yes, I do. He's so good, Tal." She put her hand on Joly. "And that's not even the reason why you like him."

"Sometimes I don't follow you at all."

"Great skill is extremely magnetic. For the lack of a better term, sexy."

I thought about it. "So is that what accounts for the horse show groupies falling all over some riders?"

"Yes, Tal, it is."

"I'm of course very proud of Lockie and all that he's accomplished but you're right, that's not why I like him."

"Then, why?"

"Probably for the qualities that make him a good trainer. He's kind, patient, intelligent. He's not self-centered, he never complains. And he thinks I have potential. Like with McStudly, he can see into the future. Lockie can sense what's hidden or undeveloped."

81

"The exact opposite reasons why my mother married Dad."

"Pretty much."

"And the exact reasons why your mother loved him."

"She loved The Swope Foundation and the good works he was trying to do through it. She loved his generous nature, how deeply he cared. I think that she loved his tenacity, that even when she pushed him away, he didn't give up."

"Did she really want him to stay away or was it a test?"

"No, she really wanted him out of our lives. He had to win her back. I didn't understand it then. Now I understand it a little better."

Greer glanced at the clock. "I hope you have an easier time of your relationship than our mothers did." Greer picked up Joly and pushed back the covers.

"I hope you find a way, too."

After putting the puppy on the floor, Greer pulled on a pair of sweats. "That's a long time in the future."

"What about Cam?"

Greer shrugged. "I don't have anything to offer him."

I got out of bed. "Don't sell yourself short."

Greer smiled ruefully. "Cam is one of those riders with horse show groupies following after him."

"I don't believe it."

"I was in Florida." She pulled a sweatshirt over her head and went into the bathroom.

"You saw this?"

"He's very desirable so there was a veritable buffet of young women prepared to serve themselves to him."

"I still don't believe this of Cam."

Greer stuck her head out the door. "Gillette MacDonnell? Don't give my mother credit for making that stuff up for *Tight and Loose*."

"No, Greer. You are one hundred percent wrong."

"Talia, grow up. It's nice to think well of people but it's not good for you to...have misplaced trust."

This went against everything my mother taught me.

"I like him," I said going into my bedroom to change into my barn clothes.

"I like him, too. He's a great guy. But, Talia, he's a guy. Lockie is a man." Greer slapped her thigh. "Pack in puppy." The two of them went down the hall to the stairs.

She was terrified of Cam.

***

By mid-morning, it was still drizzling, we had tacked Nassau and I gave Greer a leg up in the indoor. She picked up the reins and walked away from us.

"He's spectacular," Cap said. "That's not taking anything away from our other horses," she added quickly.

We had two barns full of beautiful, talented horses that could hold their own anywhere. This chestnut gelding was eye-catching. My hope was that he had a skill-set that could enhance Bittersweet Farm's public's presence immediately. So far, he was a question mark. Lockie didn't know much about him and this was the first time he was being ridden.

"How does he feel," I called to Greer.

"Comfortable. Like sitting on a barrel. You'll be better on him."

I was several inches taller than Greer, most of it leg, and felt at home on a horse that was round. CB was perfect for me.

This was one thing that made Lockie a better rider than any of us. He didn't have a favorite body type and was as content on a slab-sided horse as one who was broad. He assured me this is only because he had ridden so many horses. That was his way of being self-effacing and I didn't contradict him.

Greer urged the gelding into a trot and he floated around the ring.

"Wow," Cap said. "This is impressive."

I pulled the phone out of my pocket and dialed Lockie. "Hi."

"Hi. I know you're probably busy but I've got Greer on Nassau. I'll take a photo and send it to you."

"Okay. What's the problem? Does he look like a donkey?"

"No." I held the phone up as Greer trotted near us and took the photo then sent it to Lockie. "Is everything all right there?"

"Fine. My class is in about an hour."

There was a long pause.

"Geez. Tink did have a good eye for a horse. What's he like to ride?"

"Greer's riding him on the buckle right now."

"Have her pop over a fence. Take a photo of it."

"Greer, go back and forth over the crossed rails a few times then pop him over the rolltop." I took a position across from the fence.

She trotted him over the rails then cantered him toward the rolltop. He cleared it effortlessly and continued around the ring.

I sent Lockie the photo.

"One more reason I want to be home," he said.

"That's what you get for leaving," I replied.

"Harsh!"

"Is that the horse I'm supposed to be looking at?"

Startled, I turned to a young woman who was walking toward me.

She held out her hand. "Brooke Behrend from Gone To Ground."

"Hi." I shook her hand. "This is a German horse. Cap, would you go get McStudly?"

"Sure." Cap left the ring.

"McStudly?"

I smiled. "It's his stable name here. His papered name is Deep Stack and it's some kind of poker term that I can't seem to remember since I don't gamble."

Brooke watched Greer ride around the ring. "Is this one for sale?"

"No. He's an orphan."

"Excuse me?"

"His owner passed recently and left him to our trainer, Lockie Malone."

"So he wouldn't sell him."

"No. Tink wanted Lockie to have him."

"Tinker Devlin, the event rider who had the accident?"

I nodded.

"I'm sorry."

"I didn't know him but Lockie and he were friends in Germany."

Brooke couldn't take her eyes off the gelding. "He's fantastic. Is he an event horse?"

"I think he's a show jumper, but I could be wrong. This is the first time we've gotten on him."

Greer pulled up in front of us. "Do you want me to do anything else?"

"Let's have Cap hack him out and would you get on McStudly?"

"I'll be right back."

Greer left and I had to make small talk. Not one of my stronger skills.

"This is a nice barn. How long have you worked here?" Brooke asked.

"I live here. It's the family farm," I replied.

"Lucky."

"Very."

"What can you tell me about the Deep Stack horse?"

"Lockie and Cam Rafferty found him at Hialeah. He can be imposing but he's good-natured. We've had him doing flat work, going in two directions instead of just one."

"Any problems?"

"We all ride him and he's never misbehaved. We have a gelding from Florida who can turn himself inside out, but that's not in McStudly's repertoire."

Greer entered the ring and the process of selling the horse began. I would have preferred to be left out of it but Lockie wasn't available.

After about fifteen minutes, Brooke got on and rode around for another ten minutes then halted. He stood for her quietly, then she dismounted.

"Yeah. When can we have the vet do some radiographs?"

"Dr. Fortier is good about getting over here. I'll call the office and you can ask them yourself."

I led McStudly into the barn and Cap took him from me.

"I can't make the deal," Brooke said to me.

"I can't either. Sales are Lockie's province."

"When can you ship him to New Jersey?"

"Whenever the deal is finalized." I handed her the phone.

8

AS WE WERE GETTING READY FOR DINNER, I called Lockie to tell him that Dr. Fortier managed to squeeze McStudly in at the end of the day and he vetted sound.

"At least one of us has had a good day," Lockie said. "Everyone from up north is here. Counterpoint almost pinned."

"There's tomorrow."

"I wanted to make a better showing than this."

"You will."

"I'll go make the deal for McStudly. Thank you for showing him. Thank Greer for riding him. Thank Cap for helping."

"I have it covered."

"I know. Talk to you later."

After dinner, Greer and I took Joly for a walk around the pond. Neither of us said anything.

Getting into bed early, I tried to read but couldn't concentrate so turned off the light and lay down. The day was still with me.

Greer was beautiful, elegant, articulate and blond. She was smart and creative, instinctively understood what it would take to make her plans work. Her passion and dedication made people want to help because the benefit to the community was obvious.

Yet, in her mind, this wasn't reason enough for Cam to be interested in her. In the past, what she could offer was sex. Now that she wasn't offering that, Greer must have felt she was an outline of a young woman, nothing inside, no color, no substance, no qualities to engage someone's mind or emotions.

To her, men were all driven only by the physical aspect of life. Our father and Lockie were two exceptions. Cam was not. To Greer, he exemplified a guy. Whatever she had seen on the winter circuit, the unfortunate gesture of comfort he had made to her, only solidified her opinion.

I didn't believe that about Cam. He wouldn't have flown up from Florida to help Greer, knowing what she had been through and expect to wind up in bed with her.

Maybe I was naïve. Maybe I was overly optimistic about people. Maybe Greer did know more about the ways of the world than I did but this time she was wrong. Cam was good for her. I thought she knew that but the risk was too great for her to take.

What if she allowed herself to trust him, and Cam disappointed her? That would be bad but what might be worse for Greer was if she disappointed him.

My phone rang.

"Hi."

"Did I wake you up?"

"No, I was thinking."

"AKA worrying," Lockie said.

"I want Greer to know her own worth."

"She will, it'll just take a while. Egan will wire the money into the farm account by tomorrow. Send McStudly down with Pavel and Tomasz, okay?"

"In the van."

"Yes."

That was because neither Greer nor I had a commercial license to drive it. We could only use the trailers.

"Make sure there's a bill of sale and his papers in an envelope to go with him."

"And a bag of cookies."

"Of course. You can remember all that?" Lockie asked.

"No sweat."

"Sweat for me."

"That's not true."

"It only looks that way because you cover for me."

"Again. That's not true. What were you doing this evening?"

There was a pause. "Cam and I went to dinner with Sloane Radclyffe."

It was like something sour had hit my stomach. "No."

Greer had built up an animosity toward this woman. I wasn't sure they had ever met but Cam and Sloane had attended a Valentine's Day event in Napier and that had not gone over well with Greer.

"She has a horse down here and she wants Cam to ride it."

"Midnight Socialite?"

"That's the one."

"What did he say?"

"Yes. That's what catch riders say."

I had to choose my words carefully. "He's not a catch rider, he rides for Acadiana."

"Teche doesn't care as long as Cam does a good job for him."

"I don't think you understand how dicey this choice is," I replied.

"In what way?"

"Greer doesn't like her."

"What does that have to do with anything?"

"Greer. Cam. Inject the Scintillating Socialite into the mix?"

He didn't say anything for a moment. "It's business."

"Please!"

Sloane, even I knew, was very socially active on the show circuit.

"Talia, it's too late to do this. What's the problem?"

"If he sleeps with her, make sure Greer doesn't find out! It'll kill her."

"My life used to be so simple," Lockie said. "Is there something going on between them that I don't know about?"

"Semi."

"Either you do or you don't. Once you do, then there are rules. If you don't, no rules."

"It's not that cut and dried with Greer," I replied.

"It's not fair to him."

"Then he needs to leave Bittersweet and not come back."

"That's not fair to him either."

"He made that rule. He said he wasn't leaving without Remington, and Greer said Remington is not his pony any longer so forget about taking him."

"You girls are unrealistic. Talia. I have to go to sleep. I have a full day tomorrow and today was hell. Call me when you get the money and McStudly is going down the road."

I was going to stay on the important issue. "It's not fair for him to hang around being nice to her."

"Enough. Didn't I say we should stay out of their private lives?"

"She's my sister!"

"We'll discuss it on Monday. 2017."

"Lockie!"

"I'll talk to you tomorrow. Goodnight, Tal."

"Goodnight."

It took me forever to get to sleep.

***

First thing in the morning, the money for McStudly was in the account and while I packed his things, Cap was kneeling on the aisle floor, wrapping him for the trip.

"Be good," Cap told him and led him out to the van.

I was sorry to see him go. After a bit of a rough start, we all grew quite fond of him.

Pavel took the bag from me and climbed into the cab. "I will call when we arrive."

"Thank you. Have a good trip."

We waved pointlessly at the van as it went up the driveway. Cap patted me on the back. "Don't think about him again. Go ride CB, come back and we'll go to the Grill Girl for lunch."

I nodded and pulled the phone out of my pocket.

"Hi, Tal."

"The money arrived and McStudly left. I'm going to go hack CB out."

"Tal, wait."

"What."

"I'm sorry about last night."

"There's nothing to apologize for. Your opinion varies from mine, it's wrong of course, but you're entitled to it."

Lockie laughed as I hoped he would.

"You're a guy. Cam's a guy."

"McStudly is a guy."

"Yes, he is."

"We're the opposition."

"That's not it at all. You're lovely and complementary. Necessary," I said.

"I don't want to argue with you."

"Was that what we were doing?"

"Some would say so," Lockie replied.

"I wouldn't. We'll figure it out, or come to a mid-point. Greer has deeper feelings for Cam than you realize."

"I sent her home from Napier in January because I thought she would rip his head off."

I wasn't sure how to explain it. "She was hurt by his offer to take her to bed. If he now beds someone else–"

"Complicated but I get it." There was a long pause. "Do me a favor."

"Alright."

"Don't be that complicated. Or explain it to me before you get mad at me."

"I will."

"I don't know when I'll get done today but will talk to you later."

"Okay. Don't drink and ride."

He was laughing when we hung up.

I went to the lower barn to persuade Greer to ride Citabria with me and then we could all go to lunch.

***

The Zuckerlumpens arrived on time and were energetic as usual. They tacked up their ponies while Cap and I watched, but didn't help. It was important that they could do it all on their own.

Poppy spent most of the time on the aisle telling me about a movie she had seen about a girl who wanted to qualify for the Nationals and just about made it but decided it was better to have a boyfriend. Gincy and Poppy thought that was dumb and no real rider would make a choice that stupid after working so hard.

"Would you give up anything for a boy?" Gincy asked Cap.

I looked at her. "Tell us all about it, Caprice."

She gave me a smile of superiority. "The right guy would never ask you to give up anything so important to you. I have to imagine this little crumbcake wasn't very committed to her riding."

"What about you, Talia?" Poppy asked as she propped the saddle flap on top of her helmet and struggled to tighten the girth.

"I agree with Cap. Very wise advice. Fasten your helmets before you get on," I told them as we all walked to the indoor.

"What's so great about having a boyfriend," Gincy asked.

"They're good for changing tires on the trailer," Cap replied.

I gave her a thumbs up.

"I wouldn't have thought of that." Poppy led Tango to the mounting block, checked the girth and mounted.

"Here's the schedule," I started. "There's a schooling show at Red Fox Farm in two weeks. If you want to, you can go to that."

"YAY!"

"We'll go but you have to practice. I don't want as much talking and laughing when you're supposed to be working that's been going on. Now warm up."

The girls began to trot around the ring.

"You're good with them," Cap said.

"All I have to do is be the opposite of every teacher I had before Lockie," I replied.

"The tire changer."

"Genius!"

97

My phone began ringing. I dug it out of my pocket and clicked it on. "You're calling me instead of walking here?"

"I'm busy," Greer replied. "The results for the Six Year Old Jumper was just posted on the Internet. Counterpoint was pinned fifth."

"Congratulations. You must be very pleased."

"I'm happy for both of them. Lockie always shows Counterpoint to the best advantage."

"So do you," I replied.

"Yeah, okay. Talk to you later."

No sooner had I slid the phone back in my pocket when it started ringing again.

"Hi."

"I don't know what you want to do about this," Lockie said. "It's just a head's up. I just rode in the Sassafras Classis on Tropizienne and came in fourth."

"Fantastic. That's wonderful. I'm so proud of you. Not that I'm ever not proud of you but—"

"Tal, give it a rest. Cam took the class, and placed second and third."

"Clean sweep! Yay!"

"Not yay. He won on Midnite Socialite."

My stomach dropped. "Are you sure?"

Lockie laughed. "Yes. I was there to see it happen."

I grimaced. "This is not good."

When Greer found out that Cam was riding Sloane Radclyffe's horse and won a huge stakes class on it, it was going to make Armageddon look like a kindergarten field trip.

"The gentlemanly thing to say would be I wish I was there to help you see this through, but consider me a cad."

"Lockie."

"I'm expected in the ring so I'll talk to you later."

Dropping the phone to the ground and stomping on it seemed to be the best course of action but I slid it back in my pocket.

"Tal?" Cap asked.

"Enjoy the peace while we have it," I replied. "Girls. We're going to work without stirrups for the rest of the lesson."

There were groans loud enough to be heard in town.

"Independent seat, ladies. I'm concerned about your transitions. When you're asked to trot, you must begin trotting. When you're asked to canter, you don't trot-trot-trot picking up speed until you break into a canter. You go from a walk into a canter and on the correct lead."

This would be especially hard for Gincy who was staying on because of excellent balance but not a great deal of strength. Poppy had the advantage of having more time in the saddle but also had more bad habits to unlearn. So well drilled in correct position that it appeared to be a stiff pose, she needed to flow with Tango instead of sitting there like garden statuary.

It would take more than two weeks for these issues to be resolved but the Red Fox show would give them an idea where they were and where they were falling short. I hoped that would be the case, anyway. I didn't want to see them win and get the impression they didn't have to work even harder than they were.

Clapping my hands together, I began to leave the ring. "You both did a nice job today and it was an improvement over the last lesson. Take them out for a ride down the road but no farther than the end of the fence. You have to get home."

"Okay."

"Thanks, Talia," Poppy said.

Cap and I walked toward the lower barn.

"Why don't you start bringing in Butch and his pals, and I'm going to talk to Greer."

Cap turned to the field with the walk-in shed. "Good luck."

Nodding, I headed for her office.

I opened the door. "Hey. Do you have a minute?"

"Yes. I know it's a little late in the day but could we hack out a couple of the horses?" Greer asked.

"Sure." I went right up to the desk. "I don't want you finding out on the Internet."

"That Cam rode Midnite Socialite?"

"Yes. How did you find out?"

"Cam called."

"Cam called you?" I repeated, unable to believe I heard correctly.

"He said there was an offer on the table to ride for the Scintillating Socialite, trademark pending, and he wanted to know if that would have a negative impact on Bittersweet."

I was still struggling.

"It's only for Aiken," Greer said.

There was no point in dancing around the crux of the matter. "Does Sloane know that?" I asked.

"She's an heiress who's used to getting anything she wants. If she wants Cam, she's going to see this as getting her foot in the door."

"And you're okay with this?"

"What Cam does with his personal life is his business. He asked me to ride Whiskey. Why don't you get on Nassau?"

I was still stuck at the what-Cam-does-in-his-spare-time-is-his-business comment. "Nassau. We can't keep calling him that. We need a stable name. Henry?"

"Fine. Quit working and we'll ride before it gets completely dark."

Fifteen minutes later, we were walking down the dirt road, Greer on Whiskey, me on Henry.

He was a big horse and peaceful, not particularly complicated. When on the cross ties, he stood without pawing the floor. In his stall, he didn't crib or pace. If he had to be led somewhere, he followed, unlike McStudly who often was in a hurry to get to where he was going.

I wasn't sure what Henry's training had been and couldn't tell what his career was supposed to be. His personality was perfect for the farm and since he would be with us forever, that was good.

If Henry didn't have a skill-set, we could always find something for him to do. He was certainly impressive to look at, with a neck and mane that begged to be braided, we could stand him by our van for publicity photo purposes.

"Thanks, Tal," Greer said.

"For what?"

"Coming to tell me about Cam riding Sloane's horse."

"I just want you to be happy."

"Here's my advice. Choose an easier goal to achieve."

9

WHEN WE FINISHED OUR HACK and the barn chores, we went to the house for dinner.

"Hi, darling!" Victoria called from the seat at the table next to my father.

"Why are you here?" Greer asked.

"It's a social visit," she said. "And a little business."

"Here it comes." Greer picked up Joly and received kisses.

"Your father tells me the young men are in South Carolina and I did so want to see them."

"I'll bet you did," Greer replied.

"Am I to pretend I can't appreciate a handsome man simply because I'm not twenty-five?"

"Ick." I couldn't help myself, it just slipped out.

"I still appreciate your father," Victoria said and reached over to affectionately pat my father's arm.

"Stay away from him."

"It's okay, Greer," my father said. "Get cleaned up and we'll have dinner."

Greer hissed at Victoria on her way out of the kitchen.

"Do I need to ask why you need to see Lockie and Cam?" I sat in my chair.

"We need a stunt double for the Gillette character. I'm still hoping to get Adam Saunders to play the role."

Everything she said had a creepy subtext.

"So you would like to know if Cam would be interested in that job," Jules said as she brought a platter of amuse-bouches to the table.

"That's correct."

"He is a member of the Screen Actor's Guild," Jules replied. "The production company will be paying him as an actor not as a stuntman."

"You seem to know quite a bit about it." Victoria transported a small round of grilled bread layered with cheese, herbs and fresh asparagus to her mouth.

"Jules's father is in the business," I said.

Victoria chewed, swallowed then wiped her lips with the napkin. "Delicious. You could get a real job."

"This is a real job," I replied.

"That's not what I mean. Please, don't be offended. I meant you could have a restaurant or a television show."

"Or write a book," Jules added.

"Yes! My agent would love you."

Greer entered from the hallway, followed by Joly. "You're trying to take Cam and Jules away at the same time? Don't you have someone with a chateau in Burgundy to impose yourself on?"

"I'm offering them an opportunity. Just like I would offer you, darling. Would you like to be in the movie? You could be an extra. You might even get some lines. You were very good as Ophelia in the school production as I recall."

"She dies."

"Brilliantly done, too."

"You only showed up because the drama teacher was cute!" Greer said.

"Nonsense. I was there for you, darling."

"You left with him."

"Yes, we all went out for some drinks after the performance," Victoria said. "All, as in group of us. And the crime in that is..."

I grabbed the Newbury Beacon-Eagle newspaper and flipped through it until I found the local move theater listings. "Cool! Greer there's a movie at the Thaden Theater I've wanted to see. If we hurry we can just make the early show."

Greer thought.

"Lockie can't go to the movies. It's too loud for him," I explained.

105

"Yes. Let's go."

I grabbed her jacket and threw it to her then grabbed mine as we shot out the door, waving as we went. A minute later, we were in my truck headed up the driveway.

"What are we seeing?"

"What does it matter?"

"I feel bad that we stuck Dad with my mother," Greer said.

"She'll leave soon but I don't know why she keeps visiting us."

"You really don't understand?"

I turned the truck onto the main road. "Really."

"She doesn't have a boyfriend, she doesn't have a daughter, and she's stuck in this town."

I shook my head. "She made a ton of money on that book, there's a movie in the works and she could live wherever she wants. Close the door to Rowe on Main, and walk away."

"Even Victoria Kensington-Rowe has some vestigial feelings," Greer said.

After the way Greer had been treated, that she could have one iota of compassion for that woman was a surprise to me. "It's not your problem."

"No, it's not."

We reached the movie theater and looked at the lobby card.

Die Büchse der Pandora.

"What does that mean?"

"Lockie hasn't taught you German yet?"

"No, we're still working on being able understood each other in English."

Greer linked her arm through mine. "It translates to *Pandora's Box.*"

"It's in German?"

"I don't think it matters, it's a silent movie."

I sighed. "Wait. Don't they usually have subtitles? Won't those be in German?"

"Probably."

"We need Lockie," I replied as we stepped up to buy tickets.

"You're the only people in the audience this evening," the cashier told us.

"Good then we can talk the entire time. At least we won't have to worry about not being able to hear the dialog," I said as we went into the theater and found seats in the back row.

A moment later, the lights dimmed and the movie began. There was music and quite a lot of it.

"How are we supposed to talk?"

"We're here to watch."

I watched for a while and couldn't follow the action. "The actress is beautiful. Is she a–"

"Pandora's a girl who knows how to get what she wants."

I watched for a few more minutes. "Greer."

There were dancing girls with feathers and elaborate headdresses.

"Ssh. Just enjoy the movie."

"I'm bored."

"You didn't want to see this movie? Why did you drag me out of the house?"

"To get you away from your mother," I replied.

"That was very thoughtful. I have a meeting tomorrow at the Miry Brook Hunt Club. Would you like to go along?"

"For what reason?"

"Say yes or no and then we'll watch the movie."

"Yes," I said.

***

I was at my desk studying the schedule for the following day. The chores that had to be done would be pushed to the beginning and end of the day and some horses wouldn't get ridden. It wasn't so bad if some of us had a day off once in a while.

My phone rang and I checked the time. It was later than I expected. Between the movie and coming home to dinner where Jules told us everything that had happened with

Victoria after we left, the day had stretched on longer than usual.

If the normal reaction to Victoria's presence wasn't to brace for the worst, it wouldn't be so bad to have her around. Unfortunately, she did have an innate ability to create discord seemingly with no conscious awareness of it.

Jules said Victoria talked about herself and the movie for ninety minutes, then left. She and Dad had a glass of brandy and chocolate, almond, orange biscotti then called it a day.

"Where were you?" Lockie asked. "I called and it went to voice mail. You never called back."

"Greer and I went to the movies and I forgot to turn the phone back on. Victoria showed up at dinner and was being her typical self. She wants Cam to do the stunt riding for Gillette in *Tight and Loose.* She wouldn't turn down you if you expressed an interest and she offered Greer a part. Probably 'Unnamed female rider in very tight breeches'."

"Maybe they're loose breeches."

"That's not what's loose. It's the screw in Victoria's head."

Lockie laughed. "Go to sleep. I'll see you soon."

***

After our morning chores were done, we left Cap in charge, climbed into Greer's pickup truck and headed out toward Miry Brook.

"I've been talking to the head of the show committee ever since I got back from Florida. He wasn't interested in my proposal. Last month, he aged out." Greer laughed.

"He retired?"

"Yes. They decided a hundred and Pratt was old enough. Mrs. Berlin has taken over and requested a meeting based on the package. That's what this is about."

"What's the proposal?" I asked.

"Miry Brook has a spring show every year but you know attendance has been falling off because it's the same weekend as the one at Long River Equestrian Center."

I didn't actually know that, but decided to accept it as fact.

"I thought if we made the show more interesting, more people would attend and there would also be more publicity."

"I'm sorry. How are you going to make a horse show more interesting? They're all the same. Add a stakes class?"

"No," Greer said, "I thought we could make the afternoon session a Back-In-The-Day event."

"I'm lost."

"You know how working hunter classes were actually held on an outside course?"

"Yes..."

110

"We'll have a class where the riders jump out of the ring, go on the outside course, and return to the ring."

I had heard that had been done but it was before I was born.

"And people should dress in old style hunting attire."

"What? Where is anyone going to get that? They don't even make canary breeches anymore. Are you talking about those peg breeches?"

"Yes."

"Greer!"

"No, I've tracked down a number of shops carrying used clothing. If people need help, they can check the list and possibly find breeches to fit. The coat's less important."

Greer parked the truck in front of the Miry Brook clubhouse.

"No wonder the last man had reservations."

This was a very strange idea to me. It was very...she was thinking way outside the box, so far outside that she might be in another time zone.

"He was wrong," she said firmly, getting out and taking her briefcase with her.

I followed her into the building and we found the correct door, tapped and entered.

A middle-aged woman with short brown hair stood. "Greer Swope?"

"Yes. You must be Ellen Berlin."

"I am."

"This is my sister, Talia Margolin."

"I'm pleased to meet you. Sit down. My son will be here in a minute, so we won't start until he arrives." She sat behind her desk. "This is a very interesting idea you have, Greer. How did you come up with it?"

"By standing in your trophy room. I saw all the old photographs of the classic hunters and couldn't get the images out of my mind. My sister and I rode on the A show circuit. I used my equitation horse as a hunter as did Talia but shows and styles have changed. The hunters of fifty years ago are not the same as they are today."

"No."

"Every show you attend is just like the last one but at a different facility. What if it wasn't the same?"

"Hi. What do you mean the same?"

A tall young man entered the room. In a different venue, say on a fashion show catwalk, he would be a male model. Exceedingly handsome, with a perfect aquiline nose, he had ancient copper colored hair and eyes with a rust over brown tint.

"Greer Swope this is my son, Mackay. Talia Margolin, this is the numbers cruncher in the family."

"Mom," Mackay protested with a smile.

"It's true. He's always been a wiz with math. No surprise that he got a degree in finance."

He shook Greer's hand then mine. "I read the proposal. I'm sorry I don't share my mother's affinity for horses so some of the details are beyond me. I do appreciate what you did on the spreadsheet. That was difficult without knowing what parameters Miry Brook works within."

"I was able to extrapolate based on numbers I obtained from elsewhere," Greer said, then pulled a few sheets out of her briefcase and went into a lengthy explanation.

This was my sister? School had definitely been a waste of time for her. It had only held her back while Amanda was the ideal mentor because they obviously thought alike, at least where business was concerned.

Greer and Mackay discussed the number of participants the spring show had seen over the past ten years and how the Long River show had negatively impacted attendance. Even though it was across the state, it was perceived as more important because it was a three-day show with stabling. The facility was mammoth and there was always entertainment.

"If we can attract people who might have gone to Long River, or were just going to stay home because Miry Brook didn't seem to be a benefit to them, that's moving in a positive direction," Greer said.

"But it's impossible to predict," Mackay replied.

"Of course. Is it better to do nothing? We know the existing trajectory. Stay with the downward trend or try something different. My sister says," Greer turned toward me, "'He who has nothing to lose, can try anything.' What do you have to lose?"

"Advertising dollars," Mackay said. "This will be more expensive to mount than our normal spring show."

"Not necessarily." Greer fished out more pages from her briefcase. "If you bring other elements into play, the news interest will be increased and media will do a lot of the work for you. It worked with our Ambassador of Good Cheer project." Greer put more papers on Ellen's desk.

Mackay and his mother leaned over to get a better look at what Greer was demonstrating.

My phone began ringing. "I'm sorry. I should get this," I said and went into the hallway. "Lockie. You would not believe Greer."

"What's she done now?"

I thought about it for a moment. "She found herself."

***

It was after midnight when Lockie came up the stairs of the carriage house. I had left the lights on for him so he'd know I was waiting there as he had requested.

He kissed me then lay on the bed.

"Tired?"

"Yes."

"Is Mill coming back with the horses?"

"No, he's with Cap. Tracy quit."

"Excuse me?"

Lockie rolled over and propped his head up with his hand. "Greg Tolland.

"The jumper rider?"

"They have a thing for each other. Tracy said she wanted to groom for him—"

"Or groom him."

"I don't think she's been brushing out his mane. She didn't want to hurt your feelings, because everyone here has been good to her, but she wants to be with him."

"I assume she met him in Florida not three days ago."

"That's where she was on her vacation. With him." Lockie pushed himself off the bed and headed toward the bathroom.

"Are we going to lose Cap, too?"

"Teche likes Mill a lot and has plans for him. I'm not saying Mill will be here consistently but he'll be working for Acadiana for as long as he wants," Lockie called from the bathroom.

"I would miss Cap," I said.

The water started running. "Wait till I'm out of the shower!"

After today I was certain Greer would never ride with the dedication she once had. It was probably better for her to see riding and showing as a diversion than proof of her worth. There was no rush any longer. Neither of us had ever talked about riding in international competitions or the

Olympics. Maybe we both had known that once we aged out of juniors, that part of our lives was over. Some people kept going, like Nicole Boisvert, some people went to college, some found other things to do.

Greer had found something else to do.

I hadn't. I wanted to be at the barn and work with the horses. Even the Zuckerlumpens were fun.

I hoped the relationship with Greg would work out for Tracy. She was always welcome to come back.

Lockie flipped off the light in the bathroom and got into his side of the bed. "Tell me what I missed."

"Henry is a mystery. I don't know what his special power is. Do you have any idea?"

There was no answer. Lockie was asleep.

❧ 10 ❧

I LEFT LOCKIE TO SLEEP-IN and found Cap and Mill had already started feeding.

"So I hear Tracy's not coming back," Cap said.

"Is Greg Tolland cute?" I asked.

Mill looked at me. "Do I think so? He's not my type."

I shook my head. It was impossible to get a simple answer.

"He's in the Chronicle at least once a month," Cap said.

"But it's not like a portrait. The person on the horse is barely distinguishable," I replied.

"Maybe he's good—"

"Caprice..."

She gave him a look. "To travel with. You learn what a person is really like when you travel with them. Remember that time we were driving back from Palm Springs after that polo match? It was the dead of night and we had a flat tire on the trailer?"

"Yes, and your point is?"

"I knew then I could spend the rest of my life with you."

"Because I got out and changed the tire?"

"Yes. We were exhausted, it was one in the morning, and you didn't go out on the road, swearing up a storm and hurl the jack into the desert."

"The key to a successful relationship," Mill said to me.

"It is. Everything else is hype," Cap added and threw hay to Whiskey, then turned to me. "I'm not immune. Some of the hype is pretty cool, though."

I nodded. "That's why it works."

"Unlike the three of you," Mill called from the end of the aisle.

Cap and I finished our chores then we all went up to the house for breakfast.

"Where's Mr. Malone," Jules asked when we entered without Lockie.

"Sleeping."

"What time did he get in?"

"About midnight," I said and looked to Cap for confirmation.

She nodded. "Something close to that."

"It was a long day," Mill said. "I got up around four and was at the stabling area when Cam and Lockie staggered in at five."

These away shows were too demanding, although it was true Greer and I often got up at four and were headed out of the barn an hour later in past years. Pure misery to be stuck in a car with a sleepy, grumpy Greer for three hours as we were driven to the showgrounds.

"Tracy's left us for a guy with tight white breeches," I said bringing the fruit compote to the table.

"What?" Jules stopped making the waffles.

"Fooled around and fell in love," I replied.

"Maybe Victoria can get Greg to do the stunt double work on Victoria's movie. He already has the pants," Cap commented.

We laughed and went to the table.

The door opened.

"You didn't wake me up," Lockie said.

"Is that what you wanted?" I asked. "I thought you needed a couple more hours since you fell asleep while we were talking last night."

Lockie sat at his place at the foot of the table. "No. I remember having a conversation with you."

"About what?" I speared a waffle and put it on his plate.

He thought. "Tracy." He reached for the syrup. "Is that right?"

I felt Jules's foot nudge mine under the table.

"That was before you got into bed. Then I was telling you about Henry."

"And I commented quite brilliantly, if I may say so myself...Give me a hint."

"Nothing. You were practically asleep before you lay down." I handed him the bowl of deep purple fruit compote, dark berries, stone fruit, and spices simmered long enough to release all their juices and sweetness.

Lockie's eyes were bloodshot and glassy. I hoped he had taken his meds before leaving the carriage house because it was evident that Lockie had more than a little headache. Maybe he could be persuaded to take a nap after lunch.

We ate. He picked.

Tracy was my go-to girl to make sure he had water and was eating regularly when away from home. She was a great groom but so much more than just that. Now that she was gone, I was going to miss how much she helped Lockie when I wasn't there.

We finished breakfast. He couldn't hide all the food he had left and when Jules took his plate, she rested her hand lightly on his shoulder.

"Cap, will you tack up Tink's horse for me?"

She glanced toward me.

"You don't have to ask Tal," Lockie said.

Silence.

"I'm sorry I didn't mean for it to come out like that. I just want to get on him for a couple minutes."

"Sure. He'll be ready for you when you get there."

Cap and Mill left.

Lockie got up from the table, went into the bathroom and threw up breakfast. Jules and I waited for him.

"I feel better now." He took his jacket off the peg. "No, I'm not calling Dr. Jarosz." He opened the door and walked out.

"What happened?" Jules asked.

"For him shows are both business and fun. There's lots going on and when he's invited to a dinner or party, he goes. It's a way to make contacts, meet potential buyers and get recognition for our farm. That's how he sold McStudly."

"And he doesn't realize he's overdoing it," Jules replied.

"If you feel good, you keep going. Pain is your body's way of telling you to stop. But if the pain doesn't kick in until later, you're not thinking about it at the party."

"I'll make him some chicken soup."

I hugged her. "Thank you."

I went outside and he was waiting for me in the truck.

"Were you and Jules discussing me?"

"Of course. There's nothing shocking about that." I turned on the engine. "She's going to make you some chicken soup for lunch."

"There's so much for me to do, I can't afford to spend time on a fainting couch," he said sharply.

"If you had a horse who performed beautifully ninety percent of the time, but had an issue with lameness, you'd put him in a program where he could both work and rest enough to stay sound. You wouldn't whip him to do more on the days he was ouchy, would you?" I parked in front of the barn.

He opened the truck door. "Why did I get stuck with someone who's smarter than me?"

"You're such a sweet talker!" I followed him to the barn. When we got to the door, he kissed me. "I'm sorry."

"I get it."

"I know. I'll just ride Tink's horse and take the morning off."

"Okay. Then you can have lunch. If you keep that down, you can decide what the afternoon looks like."

We entered the barn.

"The Abernathys tried to hire me away from Bittersweet," Lockie said as he walked to Henry standing on the cross-ties.

"How did you forget to mention that?"

"Gee, Tal, I don't know." He circled around Henry.

"What did they offer you?"

"A ton of money. A house with a swimming pool. A budget of ten million dollars to buy show jumpers out of Europe."

I was the one feeling a bit sick. For so many years, I just got on Butch and did what I was told to do. I went to the lessons and the shows and just waited until I aged out so it would be behind me. I didn't pay attention to the investments other riders, families and farms were putting in to this process to win a blue ribbon.

Things had changed since it had become a business for us and I knew now how much money winning horses could cost. I knew Ryan Saunders' pony, Sideshow Ding, cost three hundred thousand dollars. A pony. Foxy Loxy cost nothing since he had been given to me. I spent the price of a vet exam on Garter.

An international horse? Millions of dollars. The best of everything to lure the rider to the farm.

We didn't even have a swimming pool. We had the pond. Anyone who wanted to cool off jumped in the pond including the horses. Or sitting in the stream was another alternative.

It was a lovely offer for Lockie to receive. It told me the Abernathys were convinced of his abilities and I agreed with them. Lockie was wonderfully talented. That was no surprise since he'd been working his way into the upper levels of competition since he was fourteen.

We couldn't offer him the opportunities that the Abernathys could. Even if we could, we didn't want to operate at their level. The overriding reason was that the horse world was just a diversion. A pleasant one. But it wasn't real life.

Greer was doing real life.

"Talia, come to the indoor," Lockie said as he led Henry out of the barn.

Reluctantly, I followed him out and stood by Henry's head while Lockie used the mounting block. I would always be happier if he didn't ride while he had a headache because I was unsure whether he might get dizzy. Henry would be at the farm forever. Lockie could ride him after he took a nap or even tomorrow. But that wasn't my decision to make.

"Have you been on this horse?"

"Yes," I replied. "He was very quiet. I don't know what his talents are."

They walked on the track, not on the buckle as I would, but on the bit. Lockie determining the level of training, Henry's sensitivity to aids.

"Did you try him over fences?"

"No. That's not something I would do on a horse I don't know unless you were here."

"Talia, please come here." He turned Henry toward me. I walked across the ring to them.

"Would you get on and warm him up for me?" Lockie slid off, removed his helmet, and put it on my head.

"No." I took it off and gave it back to him.

"What's this about, although I think I know, I'd like to hear it."

"If you don't feel well enough to warm up your own horse, then you shouldn't be riding. I won't help you do what goes against my conscience. If anything happened to you and I was enabling you, I couldn't live with myself. Make the wrong choice without me." I walked out of the ring, got in my truck and went up to the house.

11

JULES LOOKED AT ME in surprise as I came through the kitchen door.

"Where's Greer?"

"Her bedroom."

I went up the stairs two at a time and opened the door to her room to quickly that Joly woke from his nap and jumped to his feet.

"I'll tell you what's wrong with me," I said pacing back and forth.

"You do that and we'll see if what you think is wrong with you is what I think is wrong with you."

"My mother died too soon."

"My mother hasn't died soon enough. Next point."

"I'm serious!"

"So am I!" Greer put the cap on her pen. "What happened?"

"I'm not smart enough to deal with Lockie."

"If you can say that and mean it, you're not."

"My mother would have known what to do. She understood people. She could see into them."

"Yeah and you can't."

"I provoke people. Instead of being gentle and patient like my mother, I try to take a short cut. I think I see the right thing to do and then just rush ahead."

"What right thing did you do or not do and make it simple enough for me to understand because we're not getting it." Greer pointed to Joly.

"I have Lockie's best interests at heart but I'm perceived as being overly cautious. He wanted to ride Henry and he has a headache. I was worried that he might get dizzy. That's a long way to fall. He can't afford to hit the ground like that. He's willing to...he doesn't see it as taking a chance and I do. I was too short with him and I left him there by himself."

"Is that out of your system now?"

"Was he showing in Florida with a headache and none of you were telling me?"

Greer sighed. "Not to my knowledge."

"But he wouldn't tell you."

"You told me to be your Nanny-Cam Eyes, and I watched him. He was fine." Greer handed me some pages from her folder. "Do something productive. Read over this proposal and see if you have anything to add."

My phone rang and I looked at Greer.

"Deal with him."

It wasn't Lockie. I clicked it on.

"Tal, Lockie's down here puking his guts out," Cap said. "You might want to think about taking him to the hospital."

***

Greer sat with me in the Emergency Room waiting area after Lockie had been whisked away into a cubicle. They wouldn't let us sit with him because there were procedures.

This was churning up every memory I had of any one of the many similar experiences I had with my mother. Sudden crisis, trip to the hospital, interminable wait and the ever-present weight of fear. A little girl alone in a huge city hospital until my father arrived.

Greer took my hand. "Don't be scared."

I couldn't speak.

She squeezed my hand tightly and stood, bringing me to my feet. After checking in both directions, and seeing that, for a moment, there was no one around, Greer pulled me

127

down the corridor past the treatment areas. With only curtains, it was possible to see inside.

Lockie-no. Lockie-no. Lockie-no.

Lockie-yes.

Greer pushed past the curtain and we entered the cubicle where Lockie was laying on a gurney, an IV drip going into his hand.

He opened his eyes and looked at us. "I want to go home."

"That's enough out of you, mister. You've been plenty of trouble for one day," Greer replied.

A doctor managed to join us in the small space. "So you have some visitors. Is there a relative, or someone responsible for this wayward patient?"

"That would be me," I replied. "Talia Margolin."

"May I speak to you someplace far enough away so Mr. Malone can't overhear us?"

I nodded and followed him down the corridor to the central receiving office where he sat on the edge of the desk and I sat on a chair.

"I just spoke with Dr. Jarosz. I don't think there's much I can tell you that you don't already know. From what Lockie told us, he was in South Carolina at a horse show and engaged in social activities to the detriment of his sleep, eating and hydration. He's doing well considering his injuries in the accident."

"It could have been so much worse."

"Yes."

"Should he do less?"

"I spoke with him at length, and then with Dr. Jarosz. It doesn't occur to him to take care of himself at these sporting events, shows, whatever they are. That alert we may feel when we're pushing ourselves too hard, doesn't seem to work for Lockie as well as it should. There are medical watches people wear to remind themselves to take their meds. He could use something like that, to remind himself to drink, or eat something, or just take a rest."

"I had a groom who has been going with him to shows and Tracy was very good at monitoring him without it being obvious. But she got distracted by a boyfriend in Aiken, so my nanny wasn't there."

The doctor smiled. "This is what you're going to be dealing with. You may have some moodiness, irritability. That will tip you off that something's going on."

"He's very opinionated about his health," I replied.

"Isn't he? You're at the beginning of it. In a couple more years, you'll be experts at it. Dr. Jarosz had a message for you."

"Me?"

"He said don't worry."

"So easy to say, so hard to do."

"I know. Lockie can go home. No bucking broncos for the next twenty-four hours. Bland foods, plenty of water. I'll send you home with some Galanoactin if he still can't keep anything down. He had some already. With the fluids, he should be stable and feeling better by morning. That's about all you can do. It's not life-threatening. He told me you'd be in a panic."

"He was very talkative for someone who was feeling so lousy," I replied.

The doctor laughed. "He'll be fine. We'll let the IV finish and then he's all yours again."

"Do I want him?" I asked as we went back toward the treatment area.

"He looks like a nice enough guy, and someone with an incredibly strong will to live. After all, he survived an incident many people don't."

"I know."

We entered his cubicle and he was sitting up more than before.

"How do you feel?" I asked.

"What do I need to say in order to be kicked free?"

"Just tell the truth, you're going home anyway," I replied.

"I don't feel like throwing up."

"That's progress."

A nurse entered then removed the needle and catheter. "You're all set."

An orderly came in with a wheelchair.

"No way," Lockie said.

"Hospital policy," the nurse replied. "Get in the wheelchair or you can stay. Since you're so delightful to have around, that would be my choice."

Lockie swung his legs over the side of the gurney and the orderly helped him to the wheelchair, then he was rolled down the corridor, through the lobby and outside where Greer was waiting for us in her truck.

We got in and headed back to the farm. No one said anything until we got to the center of Newbury.

"Who's exercising the horses?"

"Cap and Cam, last I heard," I replied.

"And your name is not on the list," Greer added.

"Thank you for making that clear, I was a little confused."

"I think you're better off at the house since Jules will be there," I said, "but if you want to go to your house, I'll skip riding and can have Greer take over the Zuckerlumpens."

Lockie thought for a moment. "If I go to the main house, may I lay on your bed?"

"Of course. Take your shoes off first."

"So many rules."

"We're girls," Greer said. "You probably didn't notice."

"I noticed, trust me on that."

***

I was watching Gincy and Poppy attempt to trot over cavellettis without stirrups.

"This is impossible!" Poppy said as she struggled to maintain her position.

Gincy made another pass and it was painfully obvious how loose she was in the saddle.

"Okay. Stop. Pick up your stirrups."

"They're cute," Cam said walking up to me. "I'll ride Jetzt and head home. Or do you need me to help out?"

"Thank you. It was very thoughtful of you to offer. I think we're okay."

He turned to leave then turned back. "I don't know what this has to do with anything and I don't know if Lockie would want me saying anything."

"This lead-up sounds awful."

"Jennifer Nicholson was at the show in Aiken."

"Riding?"

"No, not yet. I've known Lockie for some years but just as someone you'd see on the circuit. Friendly but not friends. I don't know anything about his personal life or his background. I saw him at shows and then he went to Europe. When he came back, he was all about eventing so our paths didn't cross." Cam watched my pony riders trot around the arena.

"I know that Lockie and Jennifer dated at some point in the past. I know dated means slept together. What are you trying to tell me?"

132

Cam didn't look at me. "She was hanging around the Acadiana horses. She told me she wanted to talk to Teche about returning to her old job."

I could think of a hundred unpleasant things I wanted to have happen more than that.

"Teche never made it to Aiken so she was fifty shades of disappointed."

"What day was this?" I asked.

"Saturday. They had a big fight late in the day."

"How big is a big fight?"

"Big as in unpleasant and angry. I was putting Tabiche away and I heard them but don't know what was said. It wasn't 'Hot Diggity! Just who I wanted to see!' He wasn't himself after that."

"In what way?"

Cam turned to me. "Preoccupied, tired. Whatever transpired, lingered."

I watched the girls trot over the cavellettis with their stirrups. "You should be able to do that without stirrups so we know this is something to work on. You're done for the day. Why don't you take a little walk—"

"But don't go farther than the end of the fence-line because we have to go home for dinner."

"Thank you for remembering, Poppy."

The girls left the ring and I turned to Cam. "Did you eat meals with him after this incident? Did you see him drinking water? Where the freak was Tracy?"

"Tracy did her job and then scooted off to be with Greg. I'm sorry I wasn't paying that much attention but today I started thinking about it."

I nodded. "I knew Jennifer was trouble."

"Some girls are."

"Cam."

"I know you'd say the same thing about us," Cam said. "You'd be wrong, of course." He gave me a wink.

"How do we ever get along with each other?"

"Let's ask my parents. They've managed for over thirty years."

We stepped out of the indoor and stopped. Remington was out with Butch and the ponies and Cam watched them try to find one blade of new grass.

"Greer is so fond of your grandfather."

"He adores her. After she visits, he can't talk about anything else."

"I think you know more about being in a real family than we do."

"No, Tal, that's not true. My family is just as dysfunctional as yours but in different ways."

We both laughed.

12

LOCKIE SLEPT UNTIL DINNERTIME, then we all ate. Jules had made him a plain omelet and some toast so his stomach wouldn't be challenged. Afterward, Lockie and I went back to the carriage house where he was beginning to get bored with being indisposed.

"I'm riding tomorrow," he said.

"Why don't you wait to see how you feel?" I brought him a glass of water.

"I feel fine now." He took the water and didn't appear to have any intention of drinking it.

"I'm glad to hear that." I didn't believe it but getting into a disagreement about tomorrow was pointless.

He sat on the sofa. "Jennifer wants to get back with me."

"You're a very popular boy," I replied.

"Meaning?"

"The Abernathys want you, too."

"Right. I forgot about them. Swimming pool."

I nodded.

"I have a Jacuzzi here."

"Yes, you do."

There was a long silence. "Let's go to bed."

"Good suggestion."

Lockie stood, turned off the lights and I headed for the stairs.

"I'm sorry, Tal."

"About what?" I stopped halfway up the stairs.

"Today must have reminded you of other times."

"It did but Greer was there and told me not to be scared."

"Did it work?" He reached for my hand.

"A little." I continued up the stairs. "I care about you, your welfare, the things you want for yourself."

We reached the bedroom.

I removed my paddock boots. "If there's any question if you want to leave Bittersweet, you should go. You were very lucky. You were given a second chance at life. Use it."

Lockie put his arms around me. "But I am, Silly."

"Should I believe you?"

"I wouldn't lie."

"I'm not saying that. No one here would want you to feel indebted to us. We didn't give you a chance. You were hired to do a job and you did it spectacularly well. Maybe it's time to move on."

Lockie dropped his arms. "Is that what you want?"

"I want you to be fulfilled. You have a great gift with your riding. Maybe you need better horses. Maybe you need..."

"An owner."

"Yes. Someone who will buy you fabulous international horses. There is no difference between you and anyone else riding at the World Equestrian Games."

"No difference?"

I thought for an instant. "Yes, you're more talented than some."

"Is that what you think I want for myself?"

"Before Florida I wouldn't have thought so. Now I wonder if we're holding you back."

"You know as well as I do that life presents challenges and opportunity. You choose. You learn from your mistakes. You choose differently the next time. So I could be—could be—an international rider with a swimming pool, or I could be here."

"Those seem to be your choices."

"I could have the kind of life I once was moving toward or I could be here with you. You, who reminds me to drink that awful coconut water because you think it's good for me, who told Tracy to spy on me in Florida. I know you did, don't bother refuting it."

"I admit it. I'm happy I did."

"Who would be happy to see me leave if that's what I wanted."

"I wouldn't be happy, just to clarify that part. I would accept it, though."

"Why would I leave someone who wants nothing from me?"

"Don't be ridiculous. I do want something from you."

"What?"

"For you to stay here forever."

Lockie put his arms around me. "I'll stay until you get tired of me."

"Who is stupid enough to get tired of you?" I asked.

"Hmm."

He pulled me to him and kissed my lips as softly as the intimation of a whisper.

***

The next morning, Lockie was standing in the middle of the ring helping Cap with Spare when Greer entered and dropped one of our horse show lawn chairs next to his feet. "Sit."

"I walk around while I coach," Lockie replied.

138

"This week you sit or I kick your butt so hard you can't sit."

"Threats of physical coercion. Could be interesting."

"I read my mother's book. Need I say more?"

"I read your mother's book. All I can say is yahoo!"

I had to smile. He felt better so that meant I felt better. He had a modest breakfast and had been promised a more interesting lunch. Jules said she was making clear broth for him and he could have alphabet pasta or rice in it.

There was a wail of protest at that—wanting real food after not eating for twenty-four hours, he promised to drive to town for pizza at Antonio's—followed by laughter from Jules.

Now he was returning to his normal schedule even though Greer and I were trying to slow him down for another day. Lockie would have none of that because there was a show in four days. What was the point in going if no one was prepared?

I was the wrong person to ask because I would say there was no point in going. But the Zuckerlumpens had been looking forward to the show and Cap was keen to have her first outing on Spare, so we were on. I hadn't expected Lockie to insist on riding Wingspread in the pre-green hunter division. Once Lockie said he was going, then Cam insisted on going. Then it was like a party.

We were going to have a caravan of trailers and maybe the van while my preference was taking one trailer and

139

maybe two horses. Do three classes, pack up and go home. The only redeeming feature was that I was not riding. Since I had to herd cats with the girls and their ponies, it was, fortunately, impossible for anyone to expect me to oh just bring CB and hack him through a working hunter class. No, but thank you very much.

He turned to me and thought for a long moment. "Would you get on CB for me?"

"Yes. Any reason?"

"I just want to watch you ride around."

I left the indoor and came back in about ten minutes after the consumption of Henry cookies, a piece of carrot and being frisked to see if I was withholding anything else.

"Why aren't you using the dressage saddle," Lockie asked as he gave me a leg up.

"We don't like it."

I turned CB to the track.

"Wait, Tal. What do you mean 'we don't like it'?"

I shrugged. "I never got used to it and it seems dumb to trail ride in it, so I use the close contact. Why?"

"You don't like it but you said we."

"He's happier when we're not working. You know that. The dressage saddle means work, this one means it's a bye day."

"Warm him up a little while I finish with Cap."

Urging CB into a trot, we stayed on the track while Cap and Spare worked over the Emerson gymnastic— bounce,

140

one stride, bounce, one longer stride—set up to help him realize there was no reason to rush. About ten minutes later, after changing directions a couple of times and cantering, I reined back to a walk.

"Do you remember any basic dressage test?" Lockie asked.

I thought for a moment. "There's the modified one I do with the Zuckerlumpens."

"Start that."

CB and I trotted, performed a volte, and went back on the track.

"Shoulder-in at the corner."

I put my inside leg at the girth and my outside leg slightly behind it.

"Easy with the inside rein. Yes."

CB did it perfectly and I was ready to quit and give him a cookie, one I had hidden so he couldn't find it.

"Let's see you extend his trot. More. More. Leg. Yes."

We trotted down the long side of the arena.

"Walk and come over to me."

Greer sat in the chair since it was obvious Lockie wasn't going to use it.

"When is the last time you did any of that?"

"When is the last time you asked me to?"

"Are you telling me you took the whole winter off?"

"Not off. We rode and sometimes we popped over a couple fences."

"Dismount."

"What?"

"And take the saddle off, too."

I slid down to the ground and unfastened my helmet as Lockie unbuckled the girth. He pulled the saddle from CB's back, and in one easy motion was sitting on him.

"Helmet," he said.

Reaching up, I handed it to him and he pushed it on.

"You've got such a little head."

"What are you doing?" I asked as Lockie trotted away from me.

"You're not even supposed to be riding," Greer called to him, "and you're bareback."

"Thank you, Greer," Lockie replied as he asked CB for a half-pass.

In my saddle, with all the concentration I could muster, I could barely achieve some stumbling sideways. If this didn't make me feel like a complete klutz nothing would.

Lockie finished by doing tempi changes down the centerline until he reached us and halted,

"That was lovely but what did it tell you."

"That you're right. He hates the saddle."

"Isn't that swell," Greer commented. "We have a show horse who wants to be ridden bareback."

Lockie slid off. "I don't think it's only the saddle. Taking the winter off was a good idea. Too much has been asked of him."

I held out my last cookie and CB practically pushed Lockie aside to get it.

"Let's get a saddle fitter here and see if we can make Herr Geist happier. My bet is that my dressage saddle puts us farther back than he wants while your close contact saddle puts you farther forward. It only has to be millimeters for some horses. They're just sensitive."

I stroked CB's neck and he looked for another cookie.

"And maybe we can get a monoflap so there is less saddle for you. Would that make you happy?"

"Possibly." I wasn't the one who was looking for a dressage horse. I had been looking for a friend when Lockie found CB. "As long as CB is comfortable and it works for you, it's good for me."

"If only you were so easy-going in real life," Lockie replied and began walking out of the arena.

"And the doctor said to wait twenty-four hours before you rode and it's not even twenty yet!" I called after him.

"It was a suggestion," Lockie called back.

I turned to Greer. "Was it?"

"Do you think the doctor meant we were supposed to have a stop watch on him?" She picked up the chair and left it at the wall for later.

I didn't answer.

"You do."

"He needs time to recuperate and I don't know how long that is and maybe twenty-four hours was an estimation but maybe he meant thirty-six."

Greer came up alongside me, took the saddle and put it back on CB. "Lockie's fine. Get back on, I'll tack up Citabria and we'll go for a ride before lunch."

"Don't you have to work?"

"I did everything and emailed copies to Ellen and Amanda."

I nodded.

Ten minutes later, we were walking down the road. The weather was colder than expected and damp, with snow still remaining in the shadows where the sun couldn't reach. We were stuck in Mud Time.

"What do you want for your birthday?" Greer asked.

I was surprised she knew I had a birthday coming up in three weeks. She had avoided that celebration every year we had lived together at the farm.

"I have everything, don't I?"

"Would you like to borrow Joly?"

"Yes, I'd love to."

"Okay."

"You're getting off easy."

Greer paused. "Should we go out for dinner? Should we have a party at home? If we stay home, Jules will wind up doing everything but—"

"If we go out we won't enjoy the meal as much."

"She'll make a cake anyway," Greer said.

"We could help her. You, me and Cap."

"How many people are we thinking of? Family. Not my mother. Cap and Mill."

"Cam?"

"I know you don't know them very well but could we include Kate and Kerwin?"

"If you'd like."

"It's your party."

"I adore Cam—"

"Do you?" Greer asked.

"Yes."

"Why?"

"He's without artifice."

"What about his riding?"

"He's a wonderful rider," I replied.

Greer thought for a moment. "Yes, he is."

We walked on in silence, to the fence-line where the Zuckerlumpens were supposed to turn and head back and so did we.

"What else is the weekend of the Miry Brook Hunt Club show?"

"A-Rated? In state? Long River. Balanced Rock Farm in New York. Wanaque Farm in New Jersey."

"Balanced Rock has a huge stakes class, doesn't it?" Greer asked.

"I haven't looked at the prize list but yes, it's always way up there. Why?"

"It would be wonderful if Cam would ride at Miry Brook. I know it's well beneath his abilities but wouldn't he look spectacular in pegged breeches?"

"He'd look like Jay Gatsby if we could get him to slick his hair down. We could tell him it's acting. He knows about that."

"Just as long as he's not in *Tight and Loose*," Greer replied.

That was something neither of us wanted to see, and we both feared—that somehow Victoria would find a way to insert him into the movie because even if she wouldn't admit to it, we knew she had modeled the character of Gillette after Cam.

"Do you remember reading about those hunter team classes," I asked in an attempt to get Greer's mind off her mother.

"Yes! Where pairs would ride the course at the same time."

"Wouldn't it be fun to see Lockie and Cam do that?"

Greer laughed. "But I'll bet no one else would be brave enough to try it these days."

I would barely be brave enough to watch. "Is it fair to ask Cam to give up a shot at a big stakes class to tool around an outside course?" I asked.

"Probably not. And he'd be riding for Teche."

"The destination show for that weekend is Lake Placid. Acadiana will go there."

"I think that's the following weekend," Greer corrected, her mind like a spreadsheet. "If he goes to Balanced Rock, he'd be in the neighborhood."

We turned down the driveway.

"If teleportation was a real thing," I replied, "no problem."

Greer laughed. "He couldn't ride at Miry Brook and make it to New York State in the same afternoon. It wouldn't be fair to ask."

∽ 13 ∽

WE ENTERED THE KITCHEN to have lunch and found Cam and Lockie were already at the table.

"Just who I wanted to see," Greer said.

"Which one of us," Lockie asked.

"Cam. Would you ride at the Miry Brook Hunt Club Spring Show?"

"Sheesh," I said, washing my hands.

"Why would I?" he asked sensibly.

"Because we're having normal classes in the morning and..." she started.

"Abnormal classes in the afternoon," I finished for her.

"Why do you put it that way? It'll be fun."

"Shows aren't fun. They're business," Lockie said. "Isn't that right, Cam?"

"Now you confess that they're not fun for you either?" I asked him.

Lockie shook his head. "Thank you, Greer."

"I didn't dig that hole for you."

"I don't mean fun in the way you go to an amusement park. I enjoy showing and always have, but at the moment it is very much about growing our business and making a name for Bittersweet Farm."

Cam waved his hand. "What's so much fun about the Miry Brook show and what's abnormal?"

"Because we're doing retro during the afternoon session."

Cam and Lockie looked at us, baffled.

"I'm afraid to ask," Cam said. "What's retro?"

"Back In the Day. Vintage. We're going to have classes over an actual outside course. The competitors will jump out of the ring, take real jumps like stone walls and chicken coops and split rail fences, and jump back into the ring. We're going to ask or suggest people wear old style hunt outfits."

"Pegged breeches," I added.

"We might have a hunt team class."

They stared at us in disbelief.

"That sounds delightful," Jules said, bringing sandwiches to the table. "I have a dress that would be perfect to wear and a nice picture frame hat. They're in my closet in LA, of course, but I'll have my mother send them. It's a soft pink peach silk with cream silk flowers and green leaves."

149

"No," Lockie said.

"Oh yes, it's lovely," Jules replied.

"I'm sure it is but I'm not dressing up in seventy year old clothing, and in order to look like Milton Stonecroft," he said.

Going to the table, I couldn't help laughing. "Who's Milton Stonecroft?"

"He's the rider on the old style hunter in all the discolored photos, with the scrawly handwriting on the white border designating him as Milton Stonecroft 1936."

I leaned over and kissed Lockie's cheek. "You are so cute."

As I began to stand, he took my arm and pulled me closer to kiss me back.

"Let's have lunch," Jules said.

Greer sat next to Cam. "You really won't ride at this show?"

"Is there a stakes class?"

"No."

"It's not rated. There's no prize money and I'm supposed to dress up like a mannequin in a museum of ancient clothing display? I don't think so."

"It's for a good cause."

Greer was digging in. She could do it better than anyone I knew.

"Emissary of Good Will?" Cam asked as he reached for one of Jules's pressed sandwiches.

150

"Ambassador of Good Cheer."

He knew that and was teasing her I was certain.

"I'll give you twenty-five dollars. Is that good enough?" Cam asked.

"I would prefer you," Greer replied.

We all froze.

Cam smiled at Greer. "What would you like to do with me?"

"Dress you—"

"You're a very good negotiator," Cam replied.

"Tch! Dress you in the sense I will get you the breeches and you'll be responsible for putting them on yourself."

"Then definitely no." Cam took a large bite of the sandwich.

Jules's foot pressed mine under the table.

"Cameron," Greer protested.

"Lady Gracie," Cam replied. "You were so close to a yes but turned it into a no."

"Is it the clothes?"

"Are you rethinking the dressing me part?"

"No."

"Then no."

"If you don't have to wear the pegged breeches and slick your hair back like Jay Gatsby—"

Cam burst into laughter.

"We're trying to do something. Everyone goes to destination shows and the smaller shows can't compete.

151

Miry Brook Hunt Club has existed for almost a hundred years and now it's struggling. We need to bring in a crowd."

"I'm sorry, Greer. I ride for two farms. This is the kind of show I would have attended with Remington. And cleaned up, may I add. I can't take a weekend off in the middle of the season. Teche depends on me."

"What about us?" I asked.

"Do you depend on me?"

I couldn't tell if he was teasing at that point or not and decided the truth was always better than fluff. "I do."

Cam thought for a moment. "If there was absolutely nothing else to do that weekend, which is close to impossible, and I didn't have to wear the outfit or oil my hair, I might do it for you, Tal."

Greer didn't look at him after that.

***

"He was teasing you," I said.

"He was getting back at me for Florida."

"Cam isn't petty, Greer. He was just yanking your lead shank."

We entered the barn.

"I have so much to do this afternoon. Maybe I'll ride later."

"Do you want me to turn out Counterpoint?" I asked.

"Do whatever you normally do."

"He's your horse."

"He's Lockie's horse," Greer replied.

"Wingspread is Lockie's horse."

"He's a Bittersweet Farm horse then."

When she was upset, Greer withdrew. I must have worked when she was a child, at least I hoped it had protected her from the worst. But she didn't need to do that now. Everyone wanted to protect her, not hurt her, but she couldn't see it.

I followed Greer into her office. "Didn't anyone ever tease you because they liked you?"

Greer looked at me. "What do you think? And he doesn't like me. Calling me Lady."

"You are Lady Kensington-Rowe Swope. And you called him Cameron. It was good-natured bantering. Haven't you ever seen a movie where the man and woman engage in repartee?"

"I've seen movies. Which one do you mean?"

"Well...not a current one." All I could think of were new and grubby movies that I had avoided. "I'll ask Jules and we'll watch it together and you can learn how people behave when they like each other."

"I can see how people behave when they like each other, I have you and Lockie as examples, and you never talk like that to each other."

How could I begin to explain a relationship that I didn't entirely understand?

"We skipped that step," I replied.

"Why?"

"There was too much going on to engage in the flirting behavior."

Greer sat at her desk and extracted an enormous file from one of the drawers. "I've been flirted with. No good has come of it," she replied and reached for the on button to her laptop.

The door opened.

"Hi," Mackay said with a smile. "Your barn manager said you'd be here, may I come in?"

"Of course."

"I was in town, so I thought I'd stop by."

"What brought you to Newbury?" I asked, stunned that anyone would just happen to be town.

"I had lunch at the Inn with a couple clients. It's a very nice town. Prototypically New England."

"Not as much as it used to be," I replied.

"That's the trouble with time. It marches on and drags everything into the future."

"It's not always good to cooperate with that process," Greer replied.

"I can see you feel that way from your proposal. I'd like to talk with you about it. Sometimes my mother is not as realistic as I wish she'd be."

"In what way?" Greer asked.

"The entire show must be financially viable," Mackay said. "You can't argue with math."

Greer drew a section of pages from her folder and held them out to Mackay. "I think you'll find these numbers are sound."

"I'll leave you two to the business because there are horses to ride."

"Okay."

"It was nice seeing you, Talia," Mackay said as I left the office.

"I'm sure it will happen again." I closed the door behind me and walked outside.

"Who was that?" Cap asked.

"You mean the male model?"

"Yes!"

"He's not, but he is typey, isn't he?"

"I'll say."

"Where are Lockie and Cam?"

"Cam is spotting Lockie on Henry. He just got on about ten minutes ago."

We began walking to the indoor since the footing in the ring wasn't optimal yet.

"So this guy is?"

"The son of the manager of the Miry Brook Hunt Club. Mackay Berlin. He's a financial planner or something, and is supposed to make sure the show doesn't run over-budget."

155

"That's impossible with Greer around, isn't it?"

"She'll crunch numbers until they say ouch."

We entered the arena and Lockie was cantering Dinner For Ex around the ring while Cam set up some fences.

"What gets me is that it doesn't matter what horse he gets on, he's good."

"Except for CB."

"CB has issues."

Cap laughed.

"Lockie brought him to a dressage schooling show last fall. He won the class. They took him aside to say he was punching well below his weight and don't come back in that division."

"I'll bet he looked fantastic."

"Come with us in a few weeks. He's riding CB at Gibby Plains in New York."

"If you need a groom, I'll be glad to go."

"You're welcome to come along but you don't have to work," I replied.

"Who goes to a show and doesn't wind up helping out?"

"True."

Lockie and Cam were in the center of the ring discussing the fences, then Henry was turned to the track and started to trot.

"He's so huge," Cap said as the gelding went past us.

Lockie popped him over a small fence back and forth to warm up. The horse barely made it over, hanging his knees and going so slowly I almost thought he was a sonambulist.

"What special powers does this horse have?" Cap asked softly.

"If he's supposed to be an event horse, I don't see how he could gallop the cross country."

Cam hadn't finished with the course and was busily raising the rails and spreading the oxer.

"I hope these fences are for Whiskey," Cap commented, "otherwise, this could be messy."

"Yup."

"There are days when I'm very happy Mill only has to contend with swinging mallets and polo balls traveling a hundred miles an hour." Cap paused. "Not that you should be nervous."

"Right."

I was of the opinion that taking things exceedingly slow was a very good plan. This was the first time Lockie had ridden Henry. There was no reason to do anything but get a feel for him. What Cam and Lockie considered getting a feel for a horse was much different than any notion I had.

Lockie circled Henry at the entrance and steered for a plain rail fence that appeared to be about three feet six inches. That was the small one to start things out, to get Henry into the mood.

I had to remind myself that both Lockie and Cam knew what they were doing but still I held my breath as the gelding cantered up to the fence. I had no idea what to expect. He could as easily crash through it as make it over.

Henry picked up his pace, pricked his ears forward, cleared the fence, and went to the next one. The bigger the fence, the better he jumped, with his knees up and square, easily, effortlessly.

Cam raised the fences, then he and Lockie had another discussion, pointing and gesturing, but too far away for us to hear what was being said.

Lockie and Henry jumped those fences. Cam raised them to about five feet including the in and out where the out element was a huge oxer on the far side of the arena. Henry cleared them easily then Lockie pulled him to a walk and dropped the reins to the buckle.

"I think we have a jumper," he called to me.

Henry stretched his neck out and seemed to be in danger of falling asleep.

As we entered the barn, Greer and Mackay we leaving.

"We're going to town. Greer tells me there's a good coffee shop," Mackay said. "Would anyone like to join us?"

"There's coffee at the house," I said. "And fresh biscotti."

"No thanks, I still have three horses to ride," Cam said as he walked past on his way to Whiskey's stall.

"Thank you for the invite, but so do I." Lockie continued down the aisle.

"Maybe next time," Mackey replied and they walked to his expensive European car.

"Oh God," Cap said softly. "It's not like I'm psychic but I can see what's coming from a mile away."

"No," I replied. "No. No. No."

"Are you serious?"

"We cannot have issues."

Lockie paused at the cross-ties. "I'm sure whatever you're talking about is fascinating but can someone help me with this horse? He needs to be sponged and walked. And can someone get Kyff because I need to ride him before the show."

"What?"

"What?" Lockie asked.

"Kyff's not ready to show."

"Excuse me?"

I motioned him into the tack room and closed the door behind him. "I'm not trying to tell you your business."

"It seemed like it."

"He's only had two months off. That's nothing."

"Let's see where his head's at."

"I don't agree. I think it's a mistake. I ride him almost every day and he's only squealed once this month. He's not ready. Give him a chance."

"I run the barn, right?"

"Yes, of course, you do, but I have to take his side on this. Don't be angry with me."

Lockie was still for a long moment, and then smiled. "Was it hard to stand up to me?"

I didn't understand what he was asking. "Yes, very difficult."

"Good girl." He kissed my cheek. "I wanted to see if you could. We're not a team otherwise."

I felt like I could breathe again. "You weren't going to take Kyff?"

"No, but I am taking Wing." Lockie took a step toward the door.

"He's not ready either," I said.

Lockie stopped in his tracks. "Excuse me?"

"I was on a roll so I just wanted to see if I could do it again."

Lockie turned and closed the distance between us, then put his arms around me. "I've heard the hayloft is a fine and private place."

I buried my head in his neck. "Choose. Three horses to ride or snuggling with me."

"Sometimes I think..."

Lockie's sentence drifted off into the air.

"What do you think? Is something wrong?"

Lockie took a step back and shook his head. "Everything is perfect."

Not getting the perfect vibe from him, I put my hand on his arm. "We could have tea and the biscotti at the carriage house between rides."

He put his hand over mine. "Or have a picnic for everyone here."

"Whatever you would like."

14

CAP AND I put Wing, Jetzt and Spare on the aisle and wrapped them for their trip south. Cam and Lockie were going to share the driving of the van. Cap and Mill would follow in my truck.

"I never had the resources to show outside of a fifty mile radius of Old Newbury," Cap said, finishing with Spare.

I wrapped Wing's tail with a bandage so he wouldn't rub it on the way to Virginia. "If you enjoy it, there are plenty of horses you can ride and you're welcome to use Lockie's truck and trailer."

"I may take you up on that." Cap unclipped Spare from the cross-ties. "How many times do you want me to call you from the road?"

"I'll figure that everything is fine if I don't hear from you."

"I'll call when we get there. And you want me to make sure Lockie's taking care of himself."

"Without being obvious about it."

Cap grinned. "Of course."

Jules had packed our large cooler with sandwiches, fruit, juices and bottled water. They would have plenty of food for what was going to be about a six hour drive.

Choosing not to participate in the goodbye ceremony, Greer was in her bedroom working. I thought it was less about how much she had to do than it was about watching the van go up the driveway.

Cam easily climbed into the cab and rolled down the window as we led the horses into their stalls then double-checked everything. Mill and Lockie raised the ramp and locked it in place then Mill got into the passenger side of my truck.

After thinking this was such a good idea but now, faced with the reality, I wasn't so sure.

Lockie did a circuit of the van then came up to me. "I'd like to have a word with you." He walked into the barn.

I followed. "I have the list you left. I know what you want done, unless you've changed your mind."

I stopped next to him. He pushed me, slowly gently, step by step up against Wing's stall door. "I lied. I don't have anything to say." He kissed me so intensely that it was good he had me pinned, otherwise I probably would have just

163

sunk to the floor as though my bones had magically been removed.

"Don't go," I whispered when my mouth was able to work.

"Silly. I'll be back on Sunday. You won't even notice I'm gone." He dropped his hands and began to step away.

I grabbed his arm. "Lockie."

He leaned in to me until our foreheads touched. "This was your idea."

"Why does anyone listen to me? I don't know anything."

He kissed my cheek. "It was a good idea and you know everything important to know. More than I do. What do they say? Keep calm and post on the correct diagonal."

"No, it's Keep Calm and Mind the Gap."

"Is that what it is?" He took my hand and led my outside.

"We'd have to ask Greer."

"Speaking of whom, where is she?"

"I don't think she wants to see Cam leave."

Lockie smiled. "You sisters are some crazy brew. I'll call when we get there."

Cam started the engine, Lockie got in, and the two vehicles went up the drive.

A half hour later when I thought they were close to the New York State line, I teasingly texted Lockie "Come home. All is forgiven."

A minute later, I got a return text "You don't know what you're forgiving."

***

Instead of having a lesson, I took the Zuckerlumpens out on the trails. I rode Kyff, Poppy rode Beau and Gincy rode Call. We all stayed in our two-point position for most of the ride, trotting and cantering up and down the hills. I had put neck straps on the ponies so the girls would have something to grab on if they started to feel too loose. "There is no shame in that," I told them. I expected Gincy to have some trouble with Call because his experience far exceeded hers but she toughed it out and I started to think they were really becoming riders not just passengers.

We made our way back to the dirt road and headed for home.

"Why are we just showing in pony hunters?" Poppy asked, riding up alongside me.

"Why are you asking?"

"Because when I went to shows last year, I was entered in every class, pony hunters and equitation."

"That's how it was for me, too. How did you do in the equitation?"

"I pinned once in a while," Poppy admitted.

"That's why you're not entered next weekend. You stand a better chance of pinning if you show Tango well, than if you rode in the eq classes. I want it to be a positive experience for you."

"What's wrong with our equitation?" Gincy asked.

I didn't want to get into my personal issues with showing because they were little girls and didn't need to know how cold the rules could be. The past spring I had ridden in an equitation over fences class. Butch had done the course perfectly and as we were headed to the out-gate, I had leaned over to pat him for a job well done. I was marked down for that being judged on "loss of rein".

At that point, I realized for me, it was a rigged game I didn't want to play anymore. It wasn't about good horsemanship, relationship with the horse, or how well the team worked together. It was about rules. Some were arbitrary. Judging was an opinion sometimes unbiased, and sometimes not.

It was difficult enough to be judged, being told you were or were not good enough. When the decision could be whimsical—perhaps the judge preferred the color of a dark bay like Beau Peep to Calling All Comets who looked like two scoops of chocolate chip ice cream—then it became emotionally hard for little girls who didn't understand their wonderful ponies didn't have a chance simply because of their coats or breed.

I understood judges were looking for the best type. I had ridden Butch for years and he was the wrong type so there was very little hope for us to do better than third. My feelings of futility were an accurate assessment of the situation. I better understood Greer's ambivalence to the process now. She desperately wanted to be assured she was good enough while knowing being told by a stranger would never fill the need.

I wasn't enthusiastic about sending these sweet girls into the ring, loving their ponies desperately, to possibly get dinged down for the heinous act of patting their mount after a round. If other riders and trainers wanted to play that game, they were welcome to it. I was always going to choose my horse over a ribbon and wanted my Zuckerlumpens to do the same.

There was no way I was going to burden them with this possibility. "You need to work on it. You're both getting stronger and you are completely competent to show pony hunters this month. Next month, we'll see."

If it were up to me, they would never ride in an equitation class. Such things didn't exist in England, yet all the riders survived the absence of eq classes and still the country managed to produce riders like William Fox-Pitt, Scott Brash, and Charlotte Dujardin.

Spending nearly a year unlearning everything that had been drilled into me, I still had to be constantly vigilant about staying flexible in the saddle. A crest release was my default position over fences and I had to think every time to use automatic release. How Lockie managed to abandon everything he had gone through to get to the Medal and Maclay was a testament to his abilities.

"I'd like to ride in the Olympics," Gincy said. "I watched it on television and on Viewtube.

"Wouldn't that be awesome?" Poppy replied. "Did Lockie ride in the Olympics?"

"Not yet." How could one question fill me with such pride and dread? "Some sports like gymnastics and ice skating are best done when the athlete is young. You don't have much time to make it to the upper levels. The great thing about equestrian sports is that age makes little difference. Experience and wisdom achieved through years in the saddle work for you. Time doesn't work against you. That Reed Kessler was the youngest member of the show jumping team in history is a great accomplishment but Hiroshi Hoketsu of Japan was the oldest Olympian at seventy-one. That's a great accomplishment, too."

"Wow. What did he ride in?" Gincy asked.

We turned down the driveway.

"Dressage. If you want the goal of riding in the Olympic Games, you have the rest of your lives to get there."

"We should start practicing now," Gincy said, sitting a little straighter in the saddle. "What should we do, Talia?"

"Acquire an independent seat. Everything else will be built on that foundation."

***

When all the chores were done, the Zuckerlumpens headed home for dinner, homework and Olympic dreams, I gave CB a cookie and went to the house for dinner. As I was changing out of my barn clothes, the phone rang.

"Hi."

"We got here," Lockie said. "No problems. The temporary stabling is very temporary. Cam and I are going to sleep here tonight and Mill and Cap will tomorrow."

"Why?"

"Don't make it into something unusual. Cam brought cots. We'll be fine."

I felt like crying. I didn't want Lockie sleeping virtually outside in March even if it was Virginia. "Will you be warm enough?"

"We have blankets."

"Horse blankets."

"Yes. Plenty of them. Don't worry. Please, Tal."

I took a deep breath. "The upside is that I don't have to picture any strange show circuit groupie getting into bed with you in the motel room."

"How else do you think I'm going to stay warm?" Lockie asked.

"What's her name and Social Security number?"

Lockie laughed. "No, you're not going to track her down and use a manure fork on her butt."

"I would."

"On me first, I assume."

"You'll get much worse than a manure fork."

Lockie paused. "Would you fight for me, Tal?"

"Your memory is worse than the doctor says. I've been fighting for you from the beginning."

"You'd be surprised at what I remember," Lockie said.

"Like?"

"The tears in your eyes when you learned Butch had to retire."

"So unfair bringing that up."

"Then you called me an idiot, so the moment wasn't as poignant as it started out."

"Are you ever going to let me forget that?"

"No."

"Why not? I feel terrible about it. I wish I could take it back."

"You'd take that away from me? I thought you were adorable. I had come to the farm thinking I was going to be babysitting two spoiled brats and found you crying because you thought you were losing your only friend. That told me everything I needed to know about you and you have never taken a step wrong since."

My throat tightened. "Come home, Lockie."

He laughed. "Soon, Silly. A couple days. You can get along without me."

I couldn't, though.

∽ 15 ∽

I STAYED AT THE CARRIAGE HOUSE, wore his tee-shirt and slept on his side of the bed. Proving myself to be the original Klingon, the next morning I buried my face in CB's neck, dismayed at how much I missed Lockie yet somehow feeling not weak but right.

"Give it a rest, Talia," Greer said as she led Counterpoint to his stall. "He'll be back in two days."

I sighed.

"No one likes needy people," she replied.

"I'm not needy."

"What do you call it?"

"Every moment is precious, Greer. Lockie is a valuable member of the family. Irreplaceable."

She rolled her eyes.

"Have you never cared about anyone so much that it would hurt you to lose them?"

"Yes. You. But I'm not going to cry about it before it happens."

I didn't know what to say. I had no idea she did anything but tolerate me.

"Find a balance. You'll be happier. Is it so enjoyable to go through separation anxiety every time he goes to a show? That's his life. He's always going to be traveling. Celebrate that he's in our lives and is so successful at expressing his talent."

"I hate it when you're so smart."

"Mackay's taking me to lunch, come with us and we'll talk about the Miry Brook show."

"You don't need me to be there."

"Are you going to add anything to the discussion? You just might, but the point is we'll be together. Sometimes you're not so quick on the uptake, Tal." Greer brought Counterpoint to his stall.

***

We met Mackay at the local Japanese restaurant, Konnichiwa, and Greer asked for a large table, knowing within minutes papers would be spread everywhere. He arrived in a perfectly tailored business suit and apologized for being a bit late. It was about four minutes.

Mackay sat and just to make conversation, told us a little about the clients he had seen that morning. They sounded to me like people Teche would enjoy.

My phone began ringing and I looked at it. "I have to get this, excuse me."

"Do you want me to order for you?" Greer asked.

"Chicken Katsu." I stood and left the table.

There was a small garden area near the entrance and I headed for that as I clicked the phone on. "Hi."

"Hi. Wing just placed third in his hunter class."

"Fantastic. Was there a lot of competition?"

"Probably about thirty horses."

"This isn't such a small show," I replied.

"A lot of people had the same idea you did," he said.

"Was it cold last night?"

"No, we were fine. Are you okay?"

"Greer says I have separation anxiety every time you go to a show and I should knock it off, so she dragged me to lunch with Mackay."

There was silence for a moment.

"Lockie?"

"Yeah, don't tell Cam."

"Wait. What?"

"He's got a burr under his saddle about this guy."

I was scrambling to stay up with this conversation. "Are you saying that Cam likes Greer?"

"Of course he likes her. He wanted to sleep with her."

"Not proof of genuine affection," I replied.

"In the way he offered it was. She just took it wrong. You're partially responsible. You keep throwing them together."

"I don't accept that characterization of my actions. She needs him. There's something he gives her no one else does."

"I hope she's not looking for it in Mackay Berlin."

Turning around, between the leaves and branches of a miniature orange tree, I could see Greer and Mackay huddled over a file folder.

"Me, too."

Numbers were safe. Business was where Greer could have control. Emotions? Cam? That was a threat. That was unpredictable. It made her uncomfortable.

"I have to go but I'll talk to you later. Call the farrier and see if you can get him to come up on Monday."

"Will you be back by then?"

"We'll be home Sunday night."

"I'll call this afternoon. Bye, Lockie."

He was gone already and I went back to the table to be a third wheel on a two-wheel bicycle. They were discussing financial matters that didn't matter to me.

I ate lunch in silence, nodding when Greer shoved a piece of paper under my nose, and planned what I was going to do with the Zuckerlumpens to prepare for the show next weekend. This would be a larger show, with more competition than the last one. If they didn't pin as well this time as they did in February, I hoped they weren't going to be crushed into insensibility like Greer once was. I had to remember to bring a box of tissues.

My trajectory had been more modest, without dreams of glory. I had never imagined myself riding in the Olympics or even the Nationals but my future seemed extremely unpredictable when Butch was given to me to take my mind off my mother.

Then Greer arrived who sucked all the aspirations out of the house. After the first few shows with Butch, I didn't expect to win. It wasn't likely I would ever pin above Greer who was so lady-like and delicate, all eyes always focused on her. The small bay hunter she had before Sans Egal, Tea Biscuit, was absolutely adorable, and was still winning every class he was entered in with his new rider.

"Maybe we could bring Tea home," I said unintentionally thinking out loud.

Greer turned away from Mackay. "What tea?"

"Your small hunter."

"Call the owner and make an offer," she replied.

Mackay smiled. "We should leave business for after lunch and enjoy our meal."

He was so cute.

He wasn't right for Greer, though. What an opportunity for her to make a huge mistake and turn to someone safely appropriate because Cam challenged her beyond the point of comfort.

We finished eating and went back to the farm. Greer and Mackay went to her office and I went to the house to drown my sorrows in the tartelettes Jules had made for dinner.

"What do you want for your birthday dinner, Dolcezza?" Jules asked.

"Your chocolate cake with the chocolate buttercream icing."

Jules sat next to me. "Would you like a seven layer cake?"

"Don't tease me," I said.

She knew that was one of my favorites.

"Who do you want to invite?"

"The family."

"And Cam?"

"And his mother and grandfather."

"Teche?"

"We should. He's been so generous and has us over so often."

"Trish and Oliver?"

"Wait, wait, wait. I don't want to give you extra work but could we have a public party and then dinner for the family?"

177

"We can do that. Or we just have dinner with the inner circle and leave the party until spring."

The farm had been very private since I had arrived. Perhaps my grandparents or great grandparents had been more social but we had been quiet. My father was more social among his acquaintances but all those events took place elsewhere. Maybe it was time to open the farm to company, once in a while.

"I invented something new today and it just might tempt Teche." Jules stood up, went to the refrigerator, and came back with a jar. "It's not perfect yet but it's close." She handed me a spoon.

I dipped it into the mixture and tasted it. "That's good. Hot bread and butter pickle relish?"

"That's right. I think the juxtaposition between the hot peppers and the sweet pickles is interesting on the palate. In the next batch I'm going to add some pickled onions and pickled garlic."

I adored her pickled garlic and the pickled onions were even better.

"Why would you make another food item for him?"

"It wasn't for Teche. I was experimenting with Cubanos for us, Tal. Cuban sandwiches traditionally contain dill pickles, meat and Swiss cheese. Greer doesn't like Swiss, she says it's sour. I wanted to come up with meatless version with Fontina.

I finished my tartelette. "What's the difference between a Cubano and a Panini? They're both pressed sandwiches."

"Not much besides the pickles," Jules admitted.

"Everything is going along pretty smoothly for a change. I hope it stays that way."

Jules nodded.

"Do you think there's any chance it will?"

She laughed. "Fifty-fifty."

"Come with us to the show next weekend," I said. "Be our horseshow mom."

"Aly Beck will be there and Jane Hamblett," Jules replied.

"Our," I repeated. "Greer and me."

Jules smiled. "Yours. I'd make a poor stand-in for the very glamorous and...imaginative Victoria. What does a horseshow mom do?"

"Hold the horses, run to the judge's booth, find misplaced numbers, locate wipes for use after the Porta-Potty and of course feed everyone."

"The ulterior motive!"

"So you'll go with us?"

"Of course."

***

The Zuckerlumpens were tacking up as I arrived in the lower barn and the moment they saw me, they ran over.

"Talia! Rogue Rhoades was arrested!" Gincy announced, excitedly.

"No!"

"Yes, it's true. That's all anyone could talk about in school today."

"Who's Rogue...Whoever?" I asked.

"Rysk?"

"Is it a band?" I never turned on the radio in my truck. I barely knew where it was.

"The greatest band ever," Poppy said and started humming a tune.

"Do I want to know what he was arrested for?"

I was afraid to find out. I didn't want these cute little girls hearing about activities totally beyond their comprehension.

"He was driving 100 miles an hour over the speed limit."

I shook my head. "I hope he was in Death Valley or wherever one goes to pull such stunts."

"The Pacific Coast Highway," Poppy replied.

From what I knew of California, how did Rogue find a time when the highway wasn't a parking lot.

"He has a Nuvolari."

"Is that a car?" I asked.

"Yes! They're handmade and super!" Gincy replied. "There's a waiting list for them. You don't go to the local car dealer and drive one home."

"I hope not if you're going to go a hundred miles an hour. What's the rush? He deserved to be arrested, and I hope he stays in jail. You need to get on your ponies and learn to stay in your saddles."

Unclipped their ponies from the cross ties, they led them to the mounting block, then we walked to the outside arena.

"Yay!" Poppy said as I held the gate for them.

With the footing in the outdoor no longer covered with snow or ice and decent weather, it was time they had a break from being inside for months. Since Red Fox Farm was further south in Connecticut, I imagined they'd easily be running two rings at the show instead of just the indoor the following weekend.

"I want to see what you'll do in the pony hunter under saddle class. Pretend you're at the show. Walk, please." I watched them go around and made mental notes. "And trot, please."

Gincy had to encourage Beau to pick up a trot and then wound up on the wrong diagonal, which she corrected quickly. Poppy and Tango trotted immediately, but both ponies were a bit too fast. It was probably the excitement of being outside as well as the breeze.

"Walk, please. And canter."

Tango gave a little buck as he started, throwing Poppy forward, and the reins slid through her fingers. It took her half-way around the ring before she got organized.

"Walk, please and come to the center of the ring."

"We didn't get to go in the opposite direction," Gincy said as she turned Beau off the track.

"Let's talk first," I replied as they lined up in front of me. "Instead of me telling you how it went, how about if you tell me?"

I was greeted by silence.

Gincy and Poppy looked at each other.

"Maybe I need to carry a stick," Gincy said.

"No sticks. No one here uses a stick," I answered.

"Not Cam? Not Lockie?" Poppy asked.

"No. Can either of you explain why not?"

Poppy thought. "Because your legs are stronger than ours?"

"That's part of it. What's the rest?"

They shook their heads.

"A stick is an artificial aid. It's a short-cut, replacing good training methods. If you need a stick, you have a bigger problem than waking your horse up."

Gincy nodded.

"I was loose at the canter departure," Poppy said.

"Yes, you were. If Tango wasn't such a gentleman, you would have been on the ground. You were lucky he didn't throw a bigger buck. Ride your horse. Don't think about being cute. Don't think about who's on the rail. Don't think about who's in the ring with you or if you'll place. You should be concerned with only one thing and that's riding your horse. Take the rail and we'll try again."

The girls had their ponies walk, trot and canter more successfully this time, then I had them return to the center of the ring for another discussion.

"What's the purpose of a pony hunter class?"

Silence.

"To show the judge that your pony has the qualities of a pony hunter. What is the judge looking for?"

They thought.

"Manners?" I asked.

"Yes!" Poppy said. "It should look like a pony you could ride on a hunt. Tango did that."

I doubted very much if some of these show ring hunters would be good on a hunt field, but those were the specs. "Yes. Way of going is one of the qualities. The judge will be looking for a quiet and mannerly pony. That means kicking at the pony behind him, or biting at the rider who passes is a big no-no. What else?"

"Doing what's asked?" Gincy sounded unsure.

"That's right, Gincy. Performance. Does the pony walk, trot and canter easily. How are we doing with these basics?"

"I wouldn't pin me," Poppy said. "I would if there wasn't a lot of competition."

"It's not about who's in the class and how expensive someone else's pony is. This is about you on your pony. Where are you in your training. That's what we're going to this show to find out."

It wasn't. Greer or I could tell them where they were and we'd save the trip to Red Fox Farm. They wanted to have fun and I wanted to make sure they did. How was I going to convince them that winning ribbons wasn't the goal?

"Lockie is a good rider, isn't he?" I asked.

"Yes!"

"And Wingspread is a good horse."

"Beautiful!" Gincy exclaimed.

"Gorgeous," Poppy added.

"Lockie called me earlier and said they pinned third in a hunter class. Do you think he was disappointed?"

They nodded.

"No, he wasn't. It was feedback on Wing's training progress."

"Wouldn't it have been better if he won? Wouldn't he have been happier?" Poppy asked.

"Why would he have been happier?"

"Because Lockie would have been the best. It's best to be the best," Gincy replied as though explaining something to me I didn't understand.

"When you take a photo with your camera it's a snapshot of that moment," I replied.

They looked at me without understanding.

"Whatever you do in a class, it's like a snapshot. It's that one moment. Everything fell together for you and you won. It doesn't tell you what happened at the last show. It doesn't predict what will happen at the next show. It was just that one class."

"Are you saying there is no best?" Poppy asked.

"You're a very smart young girl," I replied. "Cross your stirrup irons in front of you and we're going to finish out the session in two-point position. Then you can take a ride down the road."

"If there's no best," Gincy asked, grumpily, "why are we working so hard?"

"So you can be good," I replied.

***

I hacked CB out at the end of the day, going into the woods where the trails were still soft and on the downhill sides, slippery. CB picked his way carefully on the slopes and on the drier stretches, we galloped, his ears pricked forward, perhaps detecting the scent of spring and rushing to greet it.

16

THE FOUR OF US WERE PLAYING CARDS after dinner, and being beaten badly by Greer. My father was almost managing to hold his own but Jules and I were losing so pathetically that we kept getting fits of giggles. Which annoyed the card sharp.

"This is serious business," she told us, sternly.

I stopped smiling, which only made me start to laugh.

"You're not a good gambler."

"I'm not," I admitted. "I haven't been good at a game since Candyland."

My phone started to ring and I checked. "It's Lockie. Deal me out."

"Gladly," Greer replied, as I stood and left the room with Joly following me.

"Hi." I sat on one of the bottom stairs and Joly sat next to me.

"I'm at the motel and getting ready to turn in."

It was still early. "Do you feel alright?"

"Yes and you'll be relieved to know Cap is watching me like a hawk. She had two nice rounds on Spare. They get along together very well and I think they'll make a strong team."

"He's fine, Tal," Cam called in the background.

"Cap and Mill are at the stables?"

"Yes. It's not cold enough to be uncomfortable. Mill fits in. If he didn't already work for Teche, he should be working for us. He's going to Arizona the first week of April, then San Diego."

"So he's going home," I said, knowing Mill was born in California, just as Lockie had been.

"For a couple days. Then Texas. Was it Houston, Cam?"

"Huntsville," Cam replied.

"Mill loves polo," Lockie said. "It's a sport for someone as tough as he is."

I wondered if Lockie was comparing his now to his past. I imagined he was as strong as ever but not quite as tough. It was one of the realities he must have learned to accept.

"Get into bed. Tell Cam no adult channels on the cable TV."

"Talia. That's the fun of staying in a motel. Those are hidden charges, listed as Pay-Per-View. No one ever knows you weren't watching a Disney movie," Lockie replied.

"Is that true?"

"It's not like I'm showing you the receipt when I get home."

"It's a business expense. It's on the farm account. I'll see it. Or I'll get Greer to look. She'll know how to find it."

"You do that," Lockie said with a laugh. "Our last class is at eleven so we'll be leaving right afterwards and should be home by early evening."

"Drive carefully. Crazy people are on the road."

"Yes, Tal," Lockie said then paused. "*Ich vermisse dich.*"

"I miss you, too."

***

At the end of losing all the card games to Greer, we took Joly out for his evening constitutional and a walk around the pond. The sky was beginning to cloud over and no stars were visible but it would be a warmer night.

"I would like you to do me a favor," I said, looping my arm through hers.

"I would have to hear what it is first."

"If you asked me, I would just say yes."

"What could I ask you?" Greer said.

"What could I ask you that would be so burdensome?" I replied.

"People have always asked me to do things for them that weren't in my best interests."

"This isn't in your interests one way or another. Sheesh. Take a Zuckerlumpen class for me this week."

"Why?"

"It would be like a clinic. Give them a different perspective. Maybe I'm not conveying the information clearly to them. They seem confused."

"How so?"

"I want them to be good riders, not necessarily winning riders."

"What could I add?"

"You once had very high aspirations and became more realistic."

Greer watched Joly follow a scent trail through the field. "Lockie had high aspirations. I had neuroses. I had to prove something. He just rides. The only thing Lockie may want is your approval."

At first, I wasn't sure I heard her correctly. "What?"

"Don't call him tonight and ask. Let him say it in his own time if it's so. I could be wrong."

I felt an unpleasant physical reaction to this idea. "What makes you think this?"

"Unfortunately, I have quite a bit more experience with people than you do. I showed more and was in Florida with him. You're not the only one who reads people. Of course, I usually do it for self-preservation. Who could attack me next."

I pulled her closer to me. "Isn't that part of your life over?"

"That part is over, and a new part has just begun." Greer slapped her hand against her leg. "Pack in there, puppy."

Joly came running to us.

"Why don't I feel like that?"

"Because everyone loves you."

"We love you."

"It's conditional. If I behave in the right way then I'm... acceptable, but if I don't—"

I gave her arm a small yank. "This perception is so off-target."

She gave me a yank in return. "We'll see."

***

By the time the morning feed was done, it was starting to drizzle. I got on my computer and checked the weather in Virginia—overcast but not raining yet. If luck held, they would be ahead of the rain for the entire trip until reaching

New York. By late afternoon, rain was predicted for the entire region and would continue into Monday.

Greer and I rode the horses who hadn't been ridden the day before and left the Zucklumpens to their own devices in the indoor that afternoon. They didn't need me watching their every move. I had seen kids at shows who couldn't jump a cross-rail in the warm-up area without their trainer standing nearby. As a junior, I was all too happy to be left alone at a show and have our former coaches flirting with another coach instead of picking on me.

As I was just getting off Kyff, my phone rang. It was Cap and not Lockie.

"Hi. Where are you?"

"At the Sloane Radclyffe estate. I wanted to give you a heads up about it. Prepare or hide it from Greer."

"What are you doing there?"

"Dropping Cam off."

I gritted my teeth so hard, it was a surprise that a couple didn't crack.

"Sloane was at the show yesterday and offered him some kind of deal to ride Midnite Socialite."

"For the season?" I asked.

"I don't know. They're inside talking about it. We'll be late."

"Is Lockie okay?"

"He's fine. Tired. We're all tired."

"I'm sorry, of course you are. How did you do on Spare?"

"I'm just a kid from Old Newbury. I didn't have expensive lessons and up until a couple months ago, I never rode a horse as good as Spare. The competition was way past my abilities."

"Don't say that!"

"I believe in being realistic," Cap said. "That's the truth. If you want someone else to ride him, no hard feelings."

"Absolutely not. You're riding him."

"Isn't the point to go to shows and win so you get your name in the Chronicle? Good publicity and all."

"No. The point is to have a training program that puts the horse first, the rider second and we leave everything else to Lockie."

Cap laughed. "I'll see you later. Lockie just left the house."

"Call me when you're an hour away and I'll get dinner started," I said.

"Bye."

"Bye."

At least she didn't click off with no warning.

After putting Kyff in his stall, I found Greer in her office.

"Cap called," I said. "They're on their way." I walked around the room. Most offices at show barns had strings of ribbons on the walls. This had nothing.

"What are you not telling me?"

"I'm getting around to it. They dropped Cam off at Sloane Radclyffe's. She wants him to ride that Socialite horse of hers."

"I'm sure she wants him to ride something," Greer replied, putting the cap back on her pen.

"Are you upset?"

Greer almost smiled. "It's not going to happen for us. You'd like that—"

"I would."

"And you're sweet to think it but Cam and I make better casual acquaintances. I'm not ready to be in a relationship and he enjoys being a boy."

"Why does everyone keep using these popular phrases that mean nothing. Being in a relationship. Being a couple. Life doesn't need to be defined. You just live it."

"Your mother was different than Victoria."

"Yes, she was."

"My mother doesn't know how to love. She uses an eyedropper to parcel out affection. Your mother even liked me."

"She did."

"I wasn't very nice to her that time we all had tea at the Palm Court," Greer said. "I regret that."

"She said you would someday."

"Speaking of Tea. If you want her, the owner is willing to sell."

"Can we afford her?"

"It'll be McStudly money. Maybe I'll show her again. I don't know why I let that bitch trainer talk me out of her."

"I thought you wanted Sans."

"Mellissa wanted him for the commission is closer to the truth. He was always a fruitcake."

"Are you serious? You rode him beautifully."

"He was so hard to ride. I was never sure if I could trust him. That's why I never let you get on."

"You didn't want me to get hurt?"

"I didn't want to get blamed when you did!"

A year ago, I would have believed that, now I knew my sister too well. She thought if she let her true feelings show, there was the possibility of being rejected and that would be more hurt than she could bear. But it wasn't true. The energy Greer expended keeping people away, could be used to draw people near.

"Do you like Cam?" I asked.

"He's fine."

"He's very fine. Do you like him in a boy-girl way?"

"Lockie came here last summer and you two clicked. That's how it works."

"You think you did not click with Cam?"

"That's right. I think we did not click. He has thought I was ridiculous from the beginning. He calls me Lady."

I sighed. "You are one."

"I didn't ask for it and it would be better if I wasn't reminded of that side of my family. My name is Swope."

Greer paused. "You could change your name if you wanted to."

"It's a little late for that."

I liked being a Margolin. I knew I was a Swope. Everyone who mattered knew that, but keeping my birth-name was a way to remember my mother, and how brave she had been.

"No, you just start going by Swope. As long as your intention is not to defraud anyone, you can call yourself whatever you want."

"You're not getting me off the topic with a name change. Give Cam a chance. My mother used to tell me to judge the other person favorably."

"I know you believe that, but it's so dangerous. You open yourself up to being taken advantage of."

I shrugged. "It's good that you don't like him in that way because it looks like he's going to be riding for Sloane Radclyffe. She's his age. She's got a ton of money. That's never a drawback."

"And she's slept with everyone else on the circuit."

I looked at her.

"Not Lockie, of course."

"Why of course?"

"He was in Germany and then he was eventing. Do you think they had a fling at the Nationals...yeah, they could have, couldn't they?" Greer stopped. "Don't think about it!"

"Listen to me. Lockie had a life before he met me. The only thing that matters is how we are together now. And that's all you should be thinking about with Cam."

"With him having a sleep-over at the Radclyffe estate."

"That is a little bit of a bump in the road," I admitted.

"You're sweet. You found someone. It's not going to happen for me and Cam. Concentrate on your boys, take good care of them, and don't play cupid."

"Okay." Until I saw my next opportunity. "Do you want to eat now or wait for them to come home?"

"I still can't get used to how early you former colonists eat dinner," Greer replied.

"We bugged out of Europe so we didn't have to stick to your rules."

Greer shook her head. "Barely better than savages."

"That whole fork thing is hard to figure. Oh wait. You all were the last to adopt forks in Europe."

"That can't be true!"

"Eighteenth century. First was Italy. Jules told me all about it."

"The biased version, her family is Italian, you know."

"Really? Is that why you speak Italian with her?"

"That must be the reason." Greer stood. "I'll help you with the chores."

"Thanks. You know the farrier's coming tomorrow so if you have anyone who needs something done, put the name on the schedule."

Greer followed me onto the aisle where the Zuckerlumpens were just coming in from their ride.

"You're good at this," Greer said.

"At?"

"Running the barn."

I wasn't sure I was doing more than following the list Lockie had given me.

"Take the compliment, you deserve it."

Poppy exchanged Tango's bridle for his halter. "We followed the stone wall to the top of the hill. You can see the town from there," she told me.

"Yes, you can see the church steeple. It's the tallest building in Newbury. One of the oldest, too."

"The jail is also one of the oldest. And so wisely situated near the bank," Greer remarked.

"Do you need some help with the chores?" Poppy asked.

"That's a lovely offer and, yes," I replied.

Greer nodded at me. Poppy had the enthusiasm to become a real horsewoman.

***

It was after eight when the van came down the driveway. All the lights were on and we were waiting for them since Cap had called when they were ten minutes out. When

Lockie climbed out of the passenger side, I figured Mill had been driving since Lockie didn't drive at night.

Cam jumped down from the cab. "Hi."

The last person I expected to see that evening, I thought Cam was staying at the Scintillating Socialite's estate to "discuss" his showing Sloane's jumper. That must have been one quick negotiation for them to get back here practically on time.

Cap and Mill got out of my truck. She shrugged at me.

"Is there something for dinner because I haven't eaten since lunch," Cam said as he started lowering the ramp.

"I have." Lockie came over and kissed me cheek. "More later."

After unloading the horses, we made them comfortable for the night then went up to the house for dinner. Cam was in performance mode, which took the burden of conversation off the rest of us, and he described the show in great detail. Jetzt had placed in two of his young jumper classes. Considering the level of competition, that was more than expected. Wingspread had placed in the one class but had switched to a more eventing mindset and was too expressive for the judge to place in the others. Spare, distracted by everything, hadn't given Cap his full attention during any of their rounds.

About halfway through the meal, it occurred to me that this light-hearted monolog was intentional on Cam's part and suspected he was doing it for Greer. Turning her head away from the flapping plastic bag caught in the tree branches was how Cam handled Greer.

***

The rain had caught up with us by the time we shut down the day at the carriage house.

"Are you tired?"

"Very," Lockie replied.

"We'll talk tomorrow then," I said and gave his hand a squeeze.

"What's on your mind?"

"Give me the short version. What happened with Cam and the Scintillating Socialite?"

"She was at the show as a spectator. Nothing in her barn is that green." He yawned. "She has many positive attributes and uses them to her advantage but she's between boyfriends. With Cam she gets two for the price of one."

"Can't she ride her own horses?"

"She does. It's very hard to coach someone like that."

"You mean because of the money," I said.

"And influence. It's a desirable position to have. It pays extremely well and you travel in elite circles with the finest of everything provided. Can you imagine how difficult it is to say 'Sloane, give the horse a break. You're flinging

199

yourself on his ears when he's trying to jump.' Remember when you first started riding and your instructor told you to keep your foot under you?"

"Yes."

"It's still true. I can't stay awake. Pack in there, Silly."

I moved closer to him and he exhaled as he fell asleep.

***

Trying to get out of bed without disturbing him, I woke him anyway.

"The barn can wait, Tal, stay with me for a few minutes."

It was still raining, so it didn't take more than that to persuade me to snuggle against him.

"What do you want for your birthday?" Lockie asked.

"You."

"Since you already have me, I'm relieved to know I don't have to go shopping or search online for the perfect gift."

"I have everything. How could anyone want more?"

"Your family will give you something."

"I told them not to bother. Just having everyone important over for dinner will be...so unbelievable. I don't know if you can imagine how grim everything was last year.

Greer was so wound up. Our trainer had left, we had no one else."

Lockie laughed. "That couldn't have bothered you."

"You know how Greer can be. If she's miserable, she makes everyone else miserable, too. Or used to. Victoria had a boyfriend who was a partner at Lundenwic Investments. He was a good catch and Victoria paraded him mercilessly."

"Greer hated that."

"She did, especially to have him sitting next to her at my birthday dinner."

"Was Jules here yet?"

"No. She arrived in May after the restaurant where she was head chef decided to switch from modern Italian to taco burgers or something."

"There's no such thing."

He pulled me closer and I could feel his breath on my neck.

"Don't bet on it. I think they renamed it The Taco Tree. They went from quality dining to a tourist trap and instant fame practically overnight. Last I heard they were franchising it."

"They need one in Vegas."

"Bingo. That's where the clone is being built."

"Taco burgers in the supermarket frozen food aisle. Mole ice cream." Lockie laughed.

"Ice cream taco sandwiches," I replied.

"No one would be that stupid," Lockie said.

"Are you sure? Special sweet tacos. I'm not kidding. Jules took me there after school got out in June. It was one of the worse culinary experiences of my life."

"Better or worse than the tendril restaurant?"

Some time ago, we had all been dragged to Jules's ex-boyfriend's new restaurant, all ingredients sourced locally, all herbivore, the portions so miniature, we had to have dinner when we got back home. We still went out for to eat as a family, but we tried to pick a restaurant that served food instead of lawn clippings.

"There's no way to compare such inedibility," I assured him.

He was so quiet I thought he might have fallen back to sleep.

"Did you get on Kyff for me?"

"Saturday. The trails are draining pretty well so I took him out on the lower loop. I took CB on the upper. He's like a mountain goat. He's the one who should be a field hunter."

"You really like him, don't you?"

"Yes."

"Even with the swish?"

"That doesn't make any difference to me. He doesn't do it on the trails. How was Wingspread in the hunter classes?"

"He was an event horse in the hunter division."

"After all these months?"

202

"Years ago he would have been fine but now, they're not looking for a real hunter."

"That's why we're having the real hunter classes at the Miry Brook show. Wing will be able to go on an outside course and he'll shine. Maybe we'll start a new trend of non-destination shows."

"If anyone can, you two can."

"I can't take any credit for it. It's all Greer."

"You're just support staff," Lockie said.

"That's right."

"You worked with Wing the entire time I was in Florida and did it so well that, without preparation on my part, I could take him to a large show and pick up a fourth place against very strong competition."

"I just did what you told me to do."

"You did much more than that. I can show any horse that's been trained. When I left for Florida, Wing had been started. When I came back, he's ready to show. I didn't do that, you did. You're not support staff, you're a trainer."

"You don't have to compliment the boss's daughter. The job's yours for as long as you want it," I replied.

"Try to process this. I can trust you to do the right thing. Your instincts are spot-on and the horses like you. It's not a compliment, it's a statement of fact."

"Are you just trying to find a reason for my existence?"

"No, and it has nothing to do with horses."

Lockie kissed my neck so gently it felt as if a breeze had moved through my hair.

"*Ich habe dich vermisst*," I said.

"I missed you, too," Lockie replied.

***

After the farrier left, Lockie and I headed out in the van to pick up Greer's small hunter. She had spoken with the owners and they weren't interested in keeping the horse any longer. The daughter, who had been so keen on showing, was drifting away toward social activities. Yeah, what are those, I wondered.

"We should think about a gooseneck trailer and a diesel truck," Lockie said as he drove onto the highway ramp.

"What's wrong with the van?"

"It only holds three horses, so we're forced to take my trailer and sometimes Cam's. It would be good to have one rig and have our name on it, instead of my old truck and trailer and Cam's old truck and trailer."

"I like the van."

"No one in America uses them anymore."

"Not a good enough reason for me to change."

"We can keep the van. It's not costing us anything. I'm just saying think about it. We don't need this small hunter, do we?"

I looked at him.

"Do you mean I have to find that Egal horse and bring him back?"

"No, she...had nothing good to say about him."

"What do you mean?"

"Greer said he was hard to ride and borderline dangerous. That's why she never let me ride him. She said he was a fruitcake."

"That fruitcake is winning every time out with his new people. They're probably drugging him up if Greer's assessment is accurate and I see no reason why it wouldn't be."

"Poop be upon them. Drugs are no replacement for good training." I was silent for a moment. "When are you going to tell me what happened with Sloane? Cappy called me to say Sloane was romancing Cam at the show to get him to ride Socialite and you went to the estate to drop him off. Then you came back with him. Can you explain it?"

"Cam rides for Teche and he doesn't want to leave Acadiana Farm and he has his own horses at Bittersweet. He's very happy with the way things are and has no intention of changing anything."

"That's it?"

"That's it."

"Hmm."

"And he hates Mackay Berlin being in the same state as Greer."

"Sheesh. Why doesn't he tell her that?"

"Are you...be serious."

"I am being serious. She thinks he thinks she's ridiculous. If he gave her the smallest indication he—"

"Talia. Do not involve yourself in their relationship."

"She needs him."

"It's not our business."

"Why can't he just say something?"

"You don't know men very well, do you?"

"I know you."

"How should I take that?"

"We communicate. If we have something to say, we say it, like now."

Lockie pressed his lips together.

"They've gone out to dinner. He propositioned her..."

"She turned him down!"

"What? What am I missing about that?"

"Talia, Greer turned Cam down. That's not a good thing."

"It's not a good thing for her to sleep with someone she barely knows."

"She knew him for months."

"Around the barn."

"Yes, and your point is?"

I tried to put the pieces together but it was like a huge solid-color puzzle that didn't have a photo to use for hints. "Let's back up a little so I can understand. Are you telling me that while Greer felt he was treating her like a saddle slut, Cam got his feelings hurt?"

"Something like that."

The GPS told us to take the next road to the right.

"Oh God, this is a mess."

"That's what I'm saying. Stay out of it."

"Lockie—"

"No one interfered with us," he replied. "Do the same for them."

I didn't reply.

"For me."

"Temporarily."

"What does that mean?" He turned down the driveway as the GPS instructed.

"May. That's at least a month."

"Tal."

"We can have this discussion again then."

Out my window, I saw Tea in the field. Mane unpulled, tail full of burdock burrs, she had a long coat and was caked with mud. I was instantly furious. This horse deserved so much better treatment than this.

Lockie stopped the van, I jumped to the ground and strode over to the field. "Tea? Remember me?"

She picked up her head and started toward the fence.

"We're here to take you home."

***

Later in the day after everyone had left and I was making a final sweep of the barn, I found Greer crying as she pulled the burrs out of Tea's tail.

17

BY THE TIME I got into the tack room everyone was already there. Jules had packed a basket of sweet rolls, noshes and tea.

"Sorry I'm late," I said, sitting on my tack trunk. "Why aren't we having this meeting in the house."

"Because it would take two times longer and none of us has that much time to spare," Cam replied. "I have to ride four horses at Acadiana and show another one."

"Fine. What's such a big deal that we need to have a meeting about it?"

"Cam and I have been discussing this with Andrew, so none of this is a surprise to him—" Lockie started.

"Just to us," Greer slid in.

"Yes. It's a real shocker," Lockie replied. "All we're doing is stating the obvious. Cam and I needed time to see how everything fit together. I'm going to ride for Teche."

"What?" I nearly dropped my morning bun.

"Sounds like the makings of a great plan," Greer added.

"Ladies, please," Cam said. "Can you just hold the commentary until we finish explaining it. Then you can put us in the stocks."

I shrugged.

"Teche has the financial wherewithal that we don't. I can trade services so that our horses can go along to the larger shows with Acadiana."

"Will you be riding for Bittersweet, too?" Cap asked.

"Yes, of course. Cam and I will be riding for both farms."

"And no others," Cam added.

"Nothing changes except transportation," Lockie said.

"And that you will be here less," I replied.

"That's truth. You will have to take up some of the slack but I know you can."

"Why didn't you mention this before?"

"Because it was something we fit together this morning while you were out hacking Kyff," Lockie said to me. "If this is unacceptable, tell us now. It will make our lives easier and give Bittersweet greater visibility in the business."

"How do you figure that," Greer asked, "if you're riding Teche's horses?"

"I will also be riding Henry, Kyff and CB if he permits it." Lockie paused. "We're going from a family farm to a business. If you don't want that, I'm going to tell you there is no way I can make that work financially. Your father won't cover the bills. Greer, you're doing great work with the Ambassador of Cheer and your involvement in the hunt club, but that doesn't bring in any money. We have to cover you. Tal, you're super with the ponies and that is self-supporting. However, we have Butch, Foxy, Garter, Remington and Tea in addition to CB and Citabria who are doing nothing. You won't allow Kyff to be sold. Spare and Counterpoint at least show but will never be sold. How are we supposed to support all these horses?"

"This math doesn't work," Cap said.

"No. But if we get more involved with training sales horses and make a name for the farm by appearing at larger shows, we can do this," Lockie replied.

Lockie watched Greer stand and begin to walk out. "I know it's a change and I know how some of us find change very upsetting but we'll get through it."

"We all survived everything so far," Cam said. "This is not as big as some of the challenges we've faced."

"Yeah. And what if someone decides to boogie on down the road? Gets a better offer from...oh, say an heiress?" Greer stopped in front of Cam and glared at him.

"It's not going to happen," Cam replied.

Greer laughed mirthlessly. "You can't know how many times some guy has said that to me."

"Have I ever said it to you and then went down the road?"

"How do you know I mean you? Maybe I mean Lockie." Lockie looked at her in surprise.

Greer turned to me. "This is all very dependent on two virtual strangers who are not part of the family and have no reason to make good on any promises made today."

"This is my home," Lockie said and got up. "I can't see anything happening that would make me leave."

"That's the point! It's something you don't see, that none of us can see today, that takes this plan down!" Greer left the tack room.

"Does anyone else agree with Greer?" Cam asked.

"We can make other arrangements but it means selling off some of the horses and bringing the operation down to a level close to what it was when I got here last summer," Lockie said.

"Figure it out," Cam said and left with Cap following in his wake.

The barn phone rang and I picked it up. "Bittersweet Farm."

"Hi. This is Ellis Ferrers. I've been trying to reach Lockie Malone but his phone doesn't seem to work."

"Hang on, I'll see if he's here." I put the mouthpiece against my leg. "Are you here for Ellis Ferrers?"

Lockie reached out for the phone, but I pulled it away.

"Did you take your meds this morning?"

"Yes."

"Do you need to be topped off?"

"Yes."

I handed him the phone.

He put his hand over the receiver. "This is my home."

"It is." I kissed his cheek and left to get his pills.

Cam's truck was already gone when I got outside and Greer was leading Tea from the lower barn. HeShe looked a hundred percent better with hisher mane pulled to perfection and her tail brushed out.

"Did you know about this plan?" she asked.

"No. It blindsided me, too."

"This was not the right day to bring it up."

I walked alongside them, something I had never done before and watched as Greer turned Tea out in a pasture she had to know so well.

"She should go back in her original stall."

"That's where Call is."

"Call can go down with the other ponies."

"Okay."

We watched Tea trot up the hill.

"How can Lockie work for us and ride for Teche?"

"For practicality's sake," I replied. "He's not leaving."

"I know that."

We leaned over the fence and watched the horses graze on what little they could find.

"Is this plan because of Tea?" Greer asked.

"She probably didn't help. Don't feel guilty. How many horses do I have here?"

"Butch and the ponies could go back in the run-in shed. That would make room for sales horses in the lower barn."

"We'll do that. It's almost April and it's not that cold at night." I turned, then stopped. "How do you feel about Cam saying he wasn't going to ride for Sloane?"

"It would be better if he did," Greer replied and headed back to the lower barn.

I drove up to the carriage house and brought back Lockie's pills.

He kissed me. "Thank you, Tal."

After pouring some tea in a cup, I found a half of a roll and handed them both to him.

"Are you going to be able to ride for Teche and do everything here, too?" I asked as he swallowed the pills.

"You will need to help."

"He must want you quite a bit," I replied.

"Teche is just lucky he's in the neighborhood," Lockie said with a smile. "I couldn't commute, that's obvious."

"Who is Ellis Whoever."

"Ferrers. Ellis and her family saw me in Florida and Aiken and she'd like to ride with me. She aged out of juniors last year and isn't happy with her trainer."

"Do you know her?"

"Come here." He raised his arm so I could snuggle up against his side and I did. "I've probably seen her but I don't remember it. How many thousand riders aged out on January first? Now they have to find something to do with their lives. The smart ones will go to college."

"Excuse me?"

"It's not the same for you and Greer." He gave me a squeeze. "You're not trying to be professional riders. It's so hard, so competitive. They have to look for horses and owners who can afford ones good enough to win."

"Are we going to be able to keep the farm paying for itself?" I asked.

"Yes. Don't worry. Just one favor, that's all I ask. Don't collect any more horses."

***

Just after lunch, Ellis Ferrers drove in pulling her very expensive rig with her name painted on the side.

Cap and I watched her park, get out and go around the back.

"That's the difference between me and most people," Cap began. "I would never write my name on my truck or trailer."

"A little help here," Ellis called to us.

"That's another difference between me and someone like her. I would do it myself." Cap began walking to the gooseneck trailer.

I went to the tack room and found Lockie checking bridle parts. "Your one o'clock is here, Mr. In-Demand Coach."

"Are your pony riders coming here today?"

"Yes."

"I'll trade you. Help me with Ellis and I'll do a guest appearance for the...what do you call them? Zucker..."

"Lumpens."

"It's so not German." Lockie put two cheek pieces to the side.

"I so do not *sprechen sie Deutsch*."

"Just *sprechen Deutsch* in that sentence." He hung up a bridle to be cleaned.

"Is Ellis thinking of boarding the horse here?"

Lockie kissed me lightly. "I don't know what she's thinking. She's probably panicked."

"Just what we don't need."

"She can see her life flashing before her eyes. It's very difficult for some people to make the transition from juniors to real life."

I walked along side him to the doorway. "Was it hard for you?"

216

"I was too busy to notice. I'd been catching rides for about four years. There were job offers waiting as I left the Medal class."

"Is that when you went back to California?"

"No, that was the next year."

"It must have been a good offer for you to give up what you had been doing."

"They had two jumpers for me to ride. I didn't give up anything."

Wearing her best show breeches and a clean jacket, as opposed to my jacket that had been torn the day before and I slapped some duct tape over the rip, Ellis led her shiny, dark brown gelding to us. "Lockie?"

⁓ 18 ⁓

"HI ELLIS," he said while shaking her hand. "It's nice to meet you. This is Talia Margolin, Bittersweet's other trainer."

I reached out to shake her hand and she made quick work of the social niceties. What she was at the farm for was definitely not me. Ellis couldn't take her eyes off Lockie.

"There's the mounting block and we can use the outdoor arena, finally, then we can talk about what you're trying to achieve."

Ellis managed to get on her horse by herself as Cap was probably hiding and I was walking to the ring with Lockie.

"What can I do to help you?" I asked.

"Keep me company," he replied.

"It doesn't sound as though you are enthusiastic about this opportunity."

"I just got past one diva."

"Greer," I said.

"You," he corrected. "Now I take on another?"

"This diva has other things to do than watching her bat her eyes at you." I started for the gate and he grabbed my arm.

"Give a guy a break. She thinks I'm sexy. What's wrong with that?"

"Didn't we have enough shenanigans in the hayloft?"

"Not hardly," Lockie said softly. "Okay, Ellis. Warm him up. Trot him around both ways, canter until you feel him relax under you."

Ellis looked at him in confusion.

"She doesn't know what you're talking about," I whispered.

"Just do what you normally do," Lockie said with a smile.

I watched her bounce around in the saddle until it made me want to break out the industrial size container of Stuck-Tite Glue.

"Seriously," Lockie said. "Watch her."

"Seriously, I've seen hundreds of riders just like her. Go to any A show and there they are."

"You can still learn from it."

I kept my eyes on Ellis who was perched precariously near her saddle, not in any conceivable way in it. "Last year, we had that session when you showed us the video history of the forward seat."

"The night that Greer kicked my furniture around the apartment?"

"That night. "When did the bouncing start, you never did say."

"I didn't? It was in the 1980's. It's not something event riders do. Do you know what a meme is?"

I had to think about it. "It's like the hot new idea."

"If you want to be in with the right people, the best people, then subconsciously you adopt their behavior. It seems a little different, so you're not one of the old group. Now you're a new and improved version. This is the opposite of you."

Now it was my turn to look at him.

"I've never met anyone so immune to what society at large is doing."

"I'm the old and tattered version." I looked at the sleeve of my jacket.

He nodded. "Ellis, he's warmed up now. Do you know a dressage test?"

"No."

"Trot around the outside of the ring, go down the diagonal and switch directions. Circle. Midway down the side canter. Do it all in the opposite direction. Then do a square halt."

"Even the Zuckerlumpens do basic dressage tests."

"That's because you're a good teacher," Lockie replied. "The pump and bump. I think this is it but it's not written in history books yet. There was an international show jumper by the name of Ivor Astaire. He had a fantastic horse named Quantify and they won everything for a few years. He had a very distinctive style."

"What does that mean? You have no clue how he stayed on?"

Lockie nodded. "I think riders started copying his form over fences because it worked for him. Everyone wants to win, isn't that right? Now it's so many years later and so many people have been taught to ride like that, no one even questions it. Everyone is doing it so it looks right. If you have the classic position, it looks wrong."

"And you don't care."

Ellis halted almost squarely.

"Not at all. Help me put the fences up to about two-six." Lockie headed toward the plain rails while I went to the in and out. "Just walk him out Ellis, then pick up your reins and pop him back and forth over that little brush jump at the top of the ring."

"Canter? Trot?"

"It doesn't matter. Whatever you're comfortable with."

The gelding seemed like a nice horse who was putting up with quite a bit of posing from her. Her equitation was flawless. She barely moved on his back. I wasn't sure that was the point but she did it so well. As I watched her warm up over the brush, Ellis couldn't be faulted for her position.

Unless she was required to actually ride, then I assumed that would be an issue. And it was. By the end of about fifteen minutes of work and rearranging the jumps into a simple gymnastic, Ellis found it impossible to sit in the saddle and keep moving forward. She found it just as impossible to maintain her two-point position.

Annoyed, she pulled up in front of us. "How am I going to drive him forward if I'm just standing in my stirrups?"

Lockie nodded. "That's a good question. Take the rail and walk. While he's walking, you do the pump and bump but hold on because he could scoot out from under you."

Two minutes later, with predictable results, she was back glaring at us. "It doesn't work at a walk, you need to be cantering already."

"All right. Explain to me how the motion works to drive the horse forward."

"The horse feels it."

"What does he feel?"

Lockie stepped over to her, put his hand on her leg and pushed lightly. The horse moved away from her leg. "I can see the cause and effect. The horse felt your leg on his side and moved in the opposite direction. If you had closed both legs on his sides at the same time, he would know to move forward. I don't understand what aid he's feeling when you're half sitting and half in two-point."

Ellis was losing her patience with him when it should have been the other way around. "Why are we talking about this?"

"To be an effective rider, you need to use your legs and you're not. Your lower leg is nowhere near your horse."

"I had the best lessons money could buy. Years of them. I won championships everywhere."

"What would you like to do with your riding now?" Lockie asked.

"I've been showing junior jumper."

"Start with ami-owner. This is a nice horse and he'll probably do that."

"I was thinking more along the lines of open jumper," Ellis said. "I promised my father if I took a gap year, then I would go to college. It has to count or I really do have to go back to school."

"That's a plan."

I could translate Lockieisms by now. That meant as a plan it had more holes in it than a miniature golf course.

"You obviously know how to ride and train jumpers," Ellis started, "will you coach me?"

"You can leave the horse here for a month and work on your foundational skills. Then we'll see where we are. Or you can look for another trainer. There are so many good ones in the northeast."

Ellis frowned. "I want you."

Betting on that was a sure thing.

"Okay. Cap Rydell is the barn manager. She'll help you with the contract and find you a stall in the lower barn," Lockie said. "Looks like your Glitter Girls have arrived."

Aly Beck's SUV had barely stopped in front of the barn when Poppy and Gincy jumped out and ran over to the rail.

"Talia! Rogue Rhoades is out of jail!" Gincy called to me.

Ellis looked down on the girls as she rode through the gate.

"He's going to create an entire album of songs about how much he suffered during those twenty-four hours," Poppy added.

Aly shrugged.

"I can't wait," I said. "Go get your ponies and I have a huge surprise for you."

"What? What? What?" Poppy twirled in the stable yard.

Lockie laughed at her energetic antics.

"Lockie is going to watch you ride this afternoon and may give you pointers for the show."

"Awesome!" Gincy pranced to the barn.

"Are they always like this," Lockie asked me as we followed at a more sedate pace.

"Isn't it great?"

He put his arm around my shoulders. "How different my introduction to Bittersweet Farm would have been if I hadn't gotten a lecture on time-keeping the first day and instead Greer spun around in delight to have a teacher who wouldn't be trying to put his hand in her breeches."

"Tch. How would we have known that?"

"Because I have an honest face," Lockie replied.

"You have a beautiful face, I'll grant you that." I stepped away from him as we entered the barn.

"What?"

"Jules and I talked about you after you went to the apartment."

"What did you two say?"

"She said you were very handsome and I think I said you wouldn't last the month. I don't really remember. You were inconsequential to me."

Lockie put his hand over his heart. "Ouch!"

"Give him a cookie and tell him you didn't mean it," Poppy told me after listening in. "It always works with Tango."

"We're just teasing each other," I assured her then gave him a look.

Ten minutes later, I was in the middle of the ring with Lockie beside me, and the girls trotting their ponies on the track.

"Walk and canter, please." I called. "Nice, Gincy. Elbows, Poppy."

"Why am I here again?" Lockie asked.

"To help the girls."

"Tali, they don't need me. They look great."

"No, no."

"Ladies," Lockie called to them.

225

Gincy giggled.

He looked at me.

"They're little girls. You're cute."

"You don't giggle over me."

I shook my head. "I'm not a little girl."

"I can get you giggling, big girl," he assured me. "Two-point position, pony riders."

They continued cantering but in their hunt seat.

"Nice work, Tali."

"Seriously?"

"Yes. Their leg position is twice as good as Ellis's."

"They're showing in pony hunters. Is there anything you would tell them?"

"Pony riders walk and come to the center of the ring," Lockie called to them.

They faced us.

"You're going to a show in a few days."

They nodded.

"What's the most important thing to do?"

Gincy raised her hand slightly. "Keep your legs on the saddle."

"Elbows in and sit up straight," Poppy added.

"True, but there's something even more important. Have fun. You're making lots of progress and that's what this is about." Smiling, he winked at them and they both giggled.

∽ 19 ∽

LOCKIE BUILT A FIRE and we sat on the sofa until it died down. Then we went upstairs.

He was tired from riding four horses here and the two at Acadiana. I thought it was probably too much but Lockie insisted it wasn't.

Sitting on the edge of the mattress, he watched me untie my paddock boots. "Wouldn't you like a normal boyfriend?"

"What's abnormal about you?"

"Cap and Mill went out this evening. I think he said they were going for pizza and then to the movies. Wouldn't you prefer that, at least some of the time, instead of staying home? Wouldn't you like to go to a square dance?"

I started laughing. "Where did that come from?"

"Bingo?"

"Are you suggesting I need more excitement in my life?"

"More fun."

"We've gone out to dinner alone and with the family. We were in Florida together for a weekend. I don't feel as though I'm missing out on something. Actually, there are times when I do."

"See."

"When you're not here, I miss sharing the day with you. I turn to tell you something cute that CB did, then I remember you're in Florida or Aiken or Virginia."

"That's why Alexander Graham Bell invented the telephone, so you could call me."

"It's not the same," I replied. "So the answer is no, I don't want a different boyfriend. Can we go to sleep now?"

Lockie nodded.

***

"I'll trade you your truck for mine today," Greer said to me at breakfast.

Lockie had already headed over to Acadiana to ride with Cam so he could get back in time to work with Ellis after lunch. The ponies would use the indoor while Cam and Lockie schooled jumpers outside. Cap was in charge of the schedule and if she wasn't a master at it, I imagined all of us

228

would be stuck in a mammoth traffic jam with every horse on the aisle at the same time.

"Sure. Why?"

"I'm going to take Tea...I'm swearing you to secrecy. That means you especially don't tell Lockie."

"Greer, that's not good for a relationship."

"You don't even know if it applies to him or not."

"Does it?"

"No. It has nothing to do with him. Think of it more like a surprise. I would prefer not to tell you but I need your help. And Lockie's trailer."

"I'm not swearing I won't tell him."

Greer's disappointment with my stance was obvious. "Here's the plan. I want to take Tea to Bertie Warner for a lesson."

As far as I knew, Bertie had retired from riding, showing and judging well before I moved to Connecticut. It was true she was legendary in New England and beyond as one of the most knowledgeable horsewomen of the past hundred years but she was out of the business. She still kept her farm, and still had a few horses but I had never seen her at a show.

"I'm totally confused. What could she teach you that Lockie can't?"

"How to ride sidesaddle."

I stared at Greer.

"Why is that so shocking? I did it when I was a child. It shouldn't be that difficult to pick it up again."

"You're an excellent rider and I'm sure you would be good at any equestrian discipline you chose. Why the hell would you want to ride sidesaddle?"

"Talia. Miry Brook. Vintage horse show. Retro classes. Does any of this sound familiar to you?"

My mind was stuttering. "Tea has never been ridden sidesaddle."

"I have over two months. She's smart. The jumps will be low."

"You're going to jump?" I asked in amazement bordering on fear.

The idea of being unable to grip the horse's sides while galloping and leaping over split rail fences or unforgiving stonewalls while twisted sideways was as horrifying an image as I could create.

"Ladies rode to the hounds sidesaddle. That means jumping. We've seen them at Devon."

I knew that Greer had made up her mind and nothing I said would change it. "Take my truck. Take Lockie's trailer. He'll be home at noon. What if he gets here before you get back?"

"What if he doesn't get here before we get back?"

"I saw what you did. How did I get involved?"

"I need help."

"Cap's going to know we're going somewhere when she sees us load Tea into the trailer and drive away with him."

"Good point." Greer finished her mug of tea. "We'll bring Keynote with us and say we're going to the state park."

"What's Keynote supposed to do while you have a lesson?"

"He'll stand in the trailer and eat hay. What difference does it make to him where he is?"

"We have to pack everything just to pretend you're not doing what you're doing?"

"It's for charity."

I looked at her.

"The Miry Brook show is for charity."

"I'm sorry. What does that have to do with riding sidesaddle?"

"Retro, Tal. We have to offer the spectators something."

I gave up. "Fine."

A half hour later, Keynote was being roused from his reverie of hay left from breakfast and found himself in the trailer with more hay. He was happy. Greer led Tea into the other stall, clipped her to the tie and I put up the tail bar. She came around back and we lifted the ramp.

"Thank you. Let's go."

"You have to help me ride the horses on the list when we get home." I went to the driver's side. It was my truck, I should drive.

"Get Cap to help. I have a ton of work."

I reached for the key in the ignition. "So do I."

"I'll do what I can. Are you going to be this difficult every time?"

"There are more times?"

"I'm good but I'll need plenty of help to ride sidesaddle perfectly by the day of the show."

"You have to ride perfectly?" I looked in the side mirrors as the truck began going up the driveway. Everything was fine.

"Of course," Greer said. "I don't want to embarrass myself."

That was so impossible there was no point in arguing about it.

***

We made it back home about fifteen minutes before Lockie and Cam arrived. Greer was upstairs taking a shower and I had just run in to help Jules with lunch when the door opened.

"Hi," Cam said.

"Hi. Did everything go well this morning?"

Lockie nodded as he went to his chair. "Cam's going to watch Ellis for a few minutes."

Why not? Get them both involved. She'll need splints on her eyelids after flapping at the professionals so ceaselessly.

"Does she need an owner?" Cam asked as he sat in his place. "Or is she a rich girl?"

I had seen her at some shows a few years back but I wasn't familiar with her financial situation. The horse was nice and she'd had an almost top trainer so she wasn't working a part-time job to pay her way.

"Why?" I asked as Jules and I brought lunch to the table.

"We should sell her a horse," Cam replied.

Greer entered looking neat in a crimson wool sweater and clean breeches. "There's no point in offering her a horse worth a quarter of a million dollars if she can afford a tenth of that. We'd have to know how much she can spend."

"Why do horses cost more than houses?" Jules asked.

"Because a winning horse is more uncommon than a house," Cam replied.

The horse Ellis was riding was worth more than twenty-five thousand dollars but there was no point in speculating about price when no one knew if she wanted a new horse. One assumed she did because as nice as this one was, it wasn't going to do what was expected of him now.

"You can find that out," Lockie replied.

"How am I supposed to do that? Hack into her family's bank account?" Greer sat next to Cam.

Lockie reached for a sandwich. "I'm sure you can discover bits and pieces on the Internet that give us a hint."

"Who's her father? What does he do for a living? These things are easy to learn," Cam said.

"How do you know that?" Greer asked.

"My brother is always putting together backstory on the characters he might play. The more you know about someone's past, the easier it is to play their present."

All I knew was that I would not be unhappy to see the Ferrers's rig going up the driveway one last time at the end of April. We didn't need boarders. That was an income and a way to cover the immediate bills, but I didn't see how that got us ahead. Selling horses would, or should, make it possible for the farm to achieve financial stability. Maybe Cam and Lockie were right. Transform Ellis into a buyer not a boarder.

We finished our soup and sandwiches then went back to work.

By the time my Zuckerlumpens arrived, Ellis was still talking, or flirting, with Cam and Lockie, so we went to the indoor. They rode without stirrups for the flatwork, and for the fences, they used their irons. I kept it like a normal lesson because it was impossible to improve much over the next few days but, incrementally, they could become tighter. The goal was an independent seat not a blue ribbon.

I wondered what Lockie was going to do with Ellis. She was reluctant, or unwilling, to change her position and that was the foundation of Lockie's program. He took away her stirrups mid-way through the lesson and let her see for herself how dependent her seat was on her irons. It was hard to do the pump and bump without a platform for her feet. She did try to stick with her old habits but since her legs weren't accustomed to work, there was no part of the saddle she didn't butt paint. CB would have hated that, so I had to give props to her horse for being genuinely tolerant.

In a way, I felt sorry for her. My father had thrown a significant amount of money at trainers to teach us something and it was only since Lockie had arrived that we had learned anything valuable. I hoped to provide a better experience for my pony riders than Greer and I had.

"Girls. We're going to practice what you will be asked to do this weekend. Then you can go for a trail ride."

"Past the end of the fence?" Poppy asked.

"Yes."

"Yay," they said softly, knowing better than to shout near the horses.

"You'll make your circle, pick up a canter, and jump the red and white striped plain rail fence. You should be on your left lead. Go to the top of the ring and turn left. Look for the fences on the diagonal. That's the panel followed by the brush. Ride to the bottom of the ring and turn right. You should be on your right lead. Take the two fences on the track. Ride to the top of the ring, look for your fence on the diagonal, it's the green and yellow striped rails. Jump it and try to pick up your left lead. Ride to the bottom of the ring and turn left. Jump the two fences on the track. Pull up slowly and walk."

They were thinking and Gincy was pointing to the fences as she remembered the course.

"Would you like me to repeat it?"

"I've got it," Poppy replied.

"Me, too," Gincy said.

"You go first, Gincy. Keep after Beau with your legs, don't let him dawdle his way around."

She picked up her reins, jogged away from us then asked for a canter and circled. He was the perfect pony for her, a little bit sleepy so that he would never get away from her and she had to work to get a good pace out of him. In another few months, she wouldn't be working so hard. Gincy's legs would be stronger and tighter and he'd know what was expected of him.

She made it around with just one moment of forgetting which way to turn after going over the two fences on the diagonal. Reining back to a walk, she came over to us.

"Terrible? I got confused."

"You did but you worked it out without making the wrong turn. Very nice. Poppy, your turn."

Poppy and Tango jogged away, picked up a canter and with great concentration, jumped the course, then returned to the center of the ring. "Let me do it again," Poppy said.

"Why?"

"Because we messed up the lead after the second fence."

"Good girl. I'm glad you caught it. Okay. Try it again. Use your rein and your leg in the air to encourage him to land on the correct lead."

The second time as was good as it could be.

"Very nice. You two girls are so ready for this show. Tomorrow you can hack out and then prepare your ponies."

"No lesson tomorrow?" Gincy asked.

"I think you'll be fine and you have a lot of work to do. You have to clean all your tack, give your ponies a bath, and help me braid." I patted Tango's neck. "Be careful out there, it's still a little muddy in spots."

"Thank you, Talia," Poppy said.

I smiled as they left the ring.

~ 20 ~

IT WAS MIDMORNING when Cam's truck and trailer drove into the yard and he hopped out.

"Hi."

I got off CB. "Hi. What's going on?"

"I went to Pennsylvania and got a horse." He let the ramp down.

Greer and Amanda came out of the barn and headed for her car.

"What's this?"

"A new horse."

"You could lead him out of the trailer," Cam said as he stood at the horse's tail.

"Amanda and I have appointments, I can't have horse all over me," Greer replied.

"I'll let down the tail bar," I said.

Cam went around the side and got in. A moment later, a horse with a black coat that seemed to be sprinkled with gray, came out of the trailer.

"Wow." Cap came up alongside me.

"What's his name?" I asked.

"He's a Selle Francais so it's...Moon Dust in French."

"Better than Moondoggie," Cap said to me.

"*Poussière de Lune*," Greer translated for us and got into Amanda's car. A moment later, they were headed up the drive.

"You didn't get him from the socialite, did you," I asked.

"As a matter of fact, I did." Cam led him to the ring to turn him out after the long trip.

I handed Cap, CB's reins and followed.

"Why?"

"Because she doesn't want him so this is like a fire sale."

I couldn't imagine anything in Sloane Radclyffe's barn would cost less than mid-six figures.

"We're not buying him, if that's your concern."

If that was my only concern, I'd be untacking my horse.

"We're agents. We'll get him sold. Maybe to Ellis. Is Freddie here? Can she hand-graze him for a while?"

"Freddie is out on Tyr, she'll be back in a half hour."

"That'll work." Cam let Moon Dust go and the gelding trotted away.

"Did you call Sloane or did she call you?"

Cam laughed. "She called me and asked if I was interested in him."

"Or interested in her."

Cam put his arm around me. "Would that be so bad?"

"Are you serious?"

He shrugged and dropped his arm. "I have to go help Lockie with the horses at Acadiana. We'll be back in time for Ellis. Have Freddie walk him—"

We turned to the ring to watch the gelding roll.

"—and wash him. Shine him up real well. I'll get on him around two o'clock."

"Okay."

"It'll be all right. Sorry I can't get to the pony show and watch the Glitter Girls, Teche is sending me to Kentucky to look at a horse, but we'll be here for your party."

"Are you getting me anything?" I asked.

"I haven't gotten it yet. I suppose a new saddle pad wouldn't be enough."

"This is what I would like. Don't hurt Greer's feelings."

Cam laughed. "Like that's possible." He got in his truck and drove away.

With access to every male on the A show circuit, why did Sloane want Cam?

That was easy to answer. He was blond, handsome and one of the best riders there was. But could she really be serious about him beyond the surface qualities? I doubted it. It was probably more likely that she had been through all the other good ones already.

As for why he would find her good company, that was obvious. She was a multimillionaire with an enormous estate. Money, being a magnet, meant that Sloane had that in her favor. And there was always the factor that she had pick of the crop horses in her barn. If a male rider needed an owner, she was always a possibility and if that entailed activities other than riding, there was the horsing around she was so well-known for.

Now we had one of her horses, happy that he was covered in sand. What was French for mess?

I went back into the barn.

***

At one o'clock sharp, Ellis arrived and was surprised to find her horse in the stall. Apparently, she was accustomed to having a groom do all the work, and all she had to do was ride. She found Cap in the upper barn but Cap was the wrong person to explain this to in hopes that the result would be a flurry of activity to get the horse ready. No one was coddled at Bittersweet. That was part of the program.

Once Lockie showed up, Ellis's temperament improved. She became downright bearable. Not to me or Cap but for

Lockie's benefit. It didn't matter. Cap took Spare into the indoor and I spent the next half hour as her ground crew, drilling on flexibility. He was a good jumper but mostly in a straight line. Point him and go. We had to work on his turns, angles at which he approached a fence, and not getting carried away with the excitement of it all.

When we finished, Cap took him out for a hack and I went in to get the Moondoggie horse ready for Cam. He was somewhat on the pushy side, like Ellis, so perhaps they would make a good team. I had the bridle on him when Cam came down the aisle carrying his saddle.

"Thanks for getting him ready." He settled the saddle on the horse's back.

"Did you ride him ever?"

"No. I left yesterday evening, picked him up, turned around and came home."

"You haven't slept?"

Cam smiled. "That's cute. You made me feel like you care about me."

"I do care. If you didn't already have a family, you'd nearly be part of ours."

"I can think of a lot worse things," he replied and unclipped the cross-ties. "If you're not busy, you can be my ground crew."

"Right." I followed him into the indoor, passing Ellis, Lockie and Cap in the outdoor ring.

Cam pulled the horse to a halt and waited for me to get closer. "I know my family has been invited to your birthday party, and we'd love to celebrate your newly achieved majority but it's easy to find an excuse to stay away if it will be better for Greer."

"Lockie told me I wasn't supposed to insert myself into your non-relationship with my sister so I don't know how to get the point across that what she says can be the reverse of what she means."

Cam picked up the reins. "I won't tattle on you."

"Thank you."

"This is a nice looking horse, isn't it?"

"What does it do?"

"Sloane got it from someone in South America."

"A French horse born there?"

The horse picked up a trot. He was sharp, had a natural crest to his neck and when the wind blew some debris against the roof, he skittered.

"Now I know why Sloane didn't want him," Cam said, bringing him back to the track. "She likes things to be very predictable. Have you ever noticed that the way people live their lives is how they ride?"

"No, I haven't."

Cam made a volte at the top of the ring. "Are you serious?"

"Yes."

"People are comfortable with what they know. Once they get to be ten years old, they're set in their ways. Very little will change." Cam and Moondoggie trotted past me.

"Is this some kind of actor approach to playing a character?"

"It is but that's because it's true."

"Aren't we all doomed then?"

"How so?"

"We will never get past anything or grow and I can tell you that it's not true."

"You mean Greer?"

"I don't think I'm supposed to be discussing her with you but yes."

Cam reined back into a walk and immediately began cantering. "You're making my case for me. Gracie had the capacity to change by the time she was ten. Maybe that instinct was buried but it was there."

"There's no way we can prove or disprove that," I replied. "It's a theory."

"It's one that works and I'll bet it holds true for you, too."

"You're saying your character is full formed by the time you're ten."

Moondoggie and Cam cantered past me. "Yes. I'm not an exception to the rule. For me, too."

"Doesn't seem right."

Cam pulled up. "Because you believe a person can grow past their limitations."

"Yes."

"What I'm saying isn't contrary to that. People can grow and change at any age. I'm just saying that was part of their personality all along. Surely you've met people who can't learn from their mistakes."

I thought about it.

"Exactly," Cam replied. "Let's try him over a couple fences. He's supposed to be ready to go."

"Why wasn't he going then?"

"Sloane's been busy this year."

I raised the rails on the fences set for the ponies.

Too busy for her horses. No wonder she wanted to thin the herd. Or use him as bait to lure Cam to the estate.

Cam trotted the horse back and forth over a low cross-rail to warm him up. By now I was so familiar with Cam's riding, it was possible to tell this was not an easy horse to ride well. He cantered Moondoggie around the ring, picking fences to jump at random.

The gelding was a stunning horse but required a rider. I wasn't sure Moondoggie was beyond Ellis's abilities. If she did buy him, would that mean she'd stay here? That wasn't an attractive scenario but if we were a training barn that meant horses and humans, too. Maybe Ellis could be trained to do her own work and be polite to the rest of us.

As we were leaving the arena, Pavel drove the tractor past the entrance, startling Moondoggie and I had to be quick to avoid the oncoming horse.

"Sorry. He's a little flighty."

"Has he ever been shown?"

"In Argentina," Cam replied as we walked into the yard.

I didn't believe it. "How old is he?"

"Coming five."

We stopped by the fence to the outside ring and watched as Lockie finished up with Ellis.

"Do you want to get on him?" Cam called to Lockie.

"Yeah."

Ellis sat on her horse in the middle of the ring while I opened the gate.

"I'll go get your helmet, Lockie." I started jogging to the barn.

"Thanks, Tal."

There was no way I was going to let him get on that horse without his own helmet. Too many unpredictable things could happen. Maybe Moondoggie needed time to settle in, but any horse that freaked over a tractor going through the stable yard, was not to be trusted. Some things were just too common to get one's nickers in a knot over.

"Come watch Lockie ride Moon Dirt," I said to Cap and Freddie who were in the tack room.

"This is a horse who has no respect for your space," Freddie said. "He practically stepped on me ten times. Next time I'm carrying a stick."

We went out, I handed Lockie his helmet and he mounted the horse. A moment later he was trotting around the ring.

The black gelding was impressive to look at.

"What color is that? Dark grey or a black roan?" Freddie asked.

"I've never heard of a black roan. Isn't that a blue roan?" Cap asked.

"Does he look like any blue roan you've ever seen?"

"No," I replied, praying that Cam and Lockie weren't going to find the money somewhere to buy this horse.

What always surprised me was how Lockie was able to get on any horse and ride it well. He didn't have to take it to the warm-up area and spend an hour, he didn't need a week to build a relationship, he just got on and got the job done. That was the difference between him and nearly everyone else—he belonged to a very small subset of riders capable of doing that and I wasn't in that group.

Aly Beck's SUV came down the driveway, parked, the girls jumped out and ran over to us. Moondoggie took one step sideways and Lockie brought him back. I saw it because I predicted a reaction, but no one else caught it. Certainly not Ellis who was in the process of falling in love.

"Come on, you rough riders. Cap and I will make sure you get on those broncos and head out on the open range."

Poppy took my hand and skipped beside me to the barn.

***

I snugged myself as close to him on the sofa as I could get. It wasn't close enough. The day had been long and we were both tired but I had been looking forward to these minutes ever since morning.

"I think Ellis is going to take Moon Dust," Lockie said.

"What about her horse?"

"We'll sell him to a nice young girl who needs a schoolmaster."

"He'll teach someone what Ellis seemed so unable to learn," I replied.

"She is competitive," Lockie admitted. "This horse will be good for her. Silly, I rescheduled my day so I could come to the show with you."

I pressed myself tighter against him.

❧ 21 ❧

IT WAS LIKE A TAILGATE PARTY with Jules catering it. There were huge containers of coffee and tea, breakfast noshes, mid-morning snacks and cookies for the ponies. People stopped going to the food stand and came to our truck instead. There was more than enough to go around.

Poppy and Gincy had more than enough people to oversee their every move. Greer took them to the warm-up area and watched them ride while I got their numbers and Lockie talked business with other trainers.

Unlike any show Greer and I ever went to, the Zuckerlumpens had fun. They were, smiling and laughing, except when Beau stepped on Gincy's foot and I had to push him off. She didn't cry but she was annoyed with him for about five minutes until all was forgiven and forgotten.

249

Lockie caught a loose pony cantering down the lane, and her little girl was crying by the time she reached it. I felt so bad for her feeling defeated even before the show got rolling that I gave her one of Jules's human cookies in the shape of a carousel horse. They were so pretty and colorful, no one wanted to eat them, but, of course, they did.

"So this is a horse show. This is what you make such a fuss over," Jules said coming up alongside of me at the rail.

"This is a very small horse show," I replied.

"Still it's all this prancing about and winning accolades."

"We may be getting too deep," I replied.

"At one time or another, everyone in my family attended an awards show in Hollywood with my father. The first few times, it's fun. You see movie stars, there are photographers, and people mistake you for a Somebody."

"Do I have to listen to a tortured childhood story?" I teased.

"Then it becomes grim," Jules said dramatically. You see behind the pancake make-up to the heavily botoxed faces. You see the dresses and tuxedos cut to hide figure flaws. You begin to see the celebrities like something in a mortuary that should have been given a burial six weeks earlier but were lost in the cooler." Jules shuddered then began laughing.

"You poor thing, scarred for life!"

"I had a lovely childhood. That's why I turned out so well."

I hugged her. "You did."

"You did, too, Dolcezza."

Greer came up beside me. "Can we quit the hug-fest and get a little serious about the show? They're in the next class."

"I know. I'm not going to be their nanny. They have to be responsible and get themselves to the in-gate."

Greer gave me a look of disbelief. "I warmed them up. They're not here on their own."

Poppy and Gincy arrived to stand in line.

I smiled at her and held out their numbers. "They're fine. They're not like we were."

***

We came home in time for Lockie's lesson with Ellis riding Moon Dust for the first time, put the ponies away, rode everyone on the schedule, then Greer and I hacked CB and Citabria while Lockie and Cam rode Jetz and Nassau. Then we had dinner with my father, grandparents, Cap and Mill in the dining room. Everyone was in a festive mood but all I wanted to do was go to the carriage house and get into bed.

He turned off the light, and I lay my head on Lockie's shoulder.

"I think Moonie is a good horse for Ellis."

251

"Why?"

"She can afford him but not a made horse. In two or three years, he should be where she wants to be now. Disappointing for her, but most people can't afford made horses."

"What about college?"

"What does that have to do with it?" Lockie asked.

"She said this is a gap year for her. If she couldn't make it, then she'd have to go to college. It was a deal she made with her father."

"I didn't hear anything about it."

"She's been too busy flirting with you."

He gave me a squeeze. "Is that true?"

"Yes. Didn't you notice?"

"All girls act that way around me. You saw how the Glitter Girls were giggling."

I sighed.

"All girls but you. Why don't you flirt with me?"

"I'm too busy."

Lockie kissed the top of my head. "You should be so proud of your riders. Poppy and Tango winning the Pony Hunter Championship. Gincy picking up a second and two thirds. You're doing such a good job, Tal."

I had seriously considered helping them find another trainer come spring but they were too much fun. "I guess I'll have to keep going with them then."

"It would be a loss to them if you didn't."

"Are you serious?" I asked.

"You don't have any idea how good you are at this."

"You're biased."

"No."

***

The sky was dark when we woke.

"Good morning, Lockie," I said rolling over to face him.

"Happy birthday, Silly. When do you really become an adult?"

"One-seventeen this afternoon."

"Where were you born?"

"New York City."

"Was your father there?"

"Yes, he was."

There was a long silence. "I think it's time to get the day going."

***

Starting after morning chores, Cap, Greer and I took turns helping Jules prepare the feast and the two cakes,

253

because one cake wouldn't be enough and three would be too many. Cap was the most helpful since she had already worked at her mother's restaurant in California. Greer and I were fine with the basics so we stuck with the simple things and left the difficult parts to the professionals.

Knowing there was a dressage show coming up, I rode CB in the ring for twenty minutes with Lockie just watching, then he got on Wing bareback and we went out into the woods. It was a good way to spend a Sunday afternoon and I was reluctant to head home, not because I didn't love or like everyone who would be at dinner, more than being made the center of attention made me uncomfortable. If it was Greer's party, that would have been fine. Also, it would have been possible when I had enough of the festivities, I could leave. The party girl has to stay until the end. There was some kind of unwritten law about that.

I helped with the afternoon chores as always, then was greeted in the kitchen by my grandmother.

"You need to hurry. Guests will be arriving."

"Do I have to play hostess?"

"You're the birthday girl!" she replied as if that answered everything.

I stripped all my barn clothes off, got into the shower and wondered if I could stay there all night.

The shower door opened. "Come on, Tal, dry off and let me do your hair."

I turned off the water and Greer handed me a towel. "Why don't you want to do this?"

I wrapped another towel around my head. "Maybe it should have just been family."

"Next year you can plan ahead a little better," Greer replied as she walked into my bedroom, picked up Joly off the bed and held him out to me.

I took him from her and he snuggled into my neck.

"You'd invite him, wouldn't you?"

"Of course. But by that logic, I would also invite CB." I toweled my hair dry and Greer began working on it.

"Do you want the same French braid with the roll?"

"Yes, please."

"I got ribbons in our stable colors to plait through it. Is that good for you?"

I turned and she lost her grip on the braid she was starting.

"What?"

"Thank you for being my sister."

"Let's leave the crying and sentiments till later. Tomorrow maybe."

She turned me around and began again.

"So you don't hate me?"

"Of course not."

"You have the worst taste in alliances," Greer said.

22

BY THE TIME WE GOT DOWNSTAIRS, me in Jules's purple dress that I loved, and Greer in her own clothes, the Coopers had already arrived.

Cam looked up as we entered the living room. He walked over to me, leaned over to give me a kiss on the cheek and said happy birthday. Turning to Greer, he looked her over carefully. "You clean up real good, Gracie. Let me introduce my father to you. Dad."

A tall man turned and came toward us. He looked so much like Cam it was almost unnerving.

"Talia Margolin, this is my father, Fitch Cooper. Dad, this is Talia of many equestrian talents."

Fitch shook my hand.

"This is Talia's sister, Greer Swope, who Granddad adores so much as well he should."

"I have heard about both of you from Cam but my father-in-law does have a bit of a crush on Greer. I'm glad I finally came East to meet you. Happy birthday, Talia."

"Thank you."

"Come say hello to Kate," Fitch said and I moved away with him leaving Cam and Greer standing near each other in silence.

Kate and her father Kerwin had dressed for the big event and congratulated me enthusiastically on my achievement of reaching eighteen years of age as though thousands of people didn't do it quite easily every day.

I made my way around the room until I wound up next to my father and Lockie.

"You look lovely," my father said and kissed my cheek.

Cap and Jules's brought plates of amuse-bouches from the kitchen and leave them around the room for people to serve themselves. My father handled the drinks and I sunk onto the couch next to Lockie.

"Teche can't make it, there was a spice crisis he had to handle. Something about Scotch Hats."

"Scotch Bonnets, I think they are."

Lockie smiled. "That's what they were. The crop failed wherever they were growing and he has to source them elsewhere by tomorrow. He promised he'd make it up to you."

"He doesn't owe me anything," I replied.

"Don't deny him his fun."

I smiled. "Of course not."

Jules called us into the dining room where Greer had topped any decorating she had done in the past. Everything was in our stable colors of dark red, dark green and yellow—the colors of the bittersweet vines climbing over the fence-line at the road.

As we were about to sit down, the kitchen door opened and I exchanged a look with Greer.

"Happy Birthday, dear Talia!" Victoria said swooping in. "My invitation must have gotten lost in the email. Where should I sit?"

"At your kitchen table," Greer replied.

Victoria pushed a small, wrapped gift in my hands. "Who is this handsome man?" She asked looking at Fitch.

"My husband," Kate replied.

"Victoria, this is my father, Fitch Cooper," Cam said as he sat next to Greer.

"What a coincidence," Victoria exclaimed as she looked for a place to sit. "You're the director the production company is going to contact about my movie."

Fitch was confused.

"*Tight Chaps and Loose Tarts*," Victoria supplied.

He shook his head. "I'm sorry."

"It's wildly popular," Victoria said. "And wild."

"I can vouch for that, Dad," Cam said.

"You said you didn't read it."

Cam turned toward Greer. "You said you did. If you did, why shouldn't I?"

"Because—" Greer started then stopped. "Excuse me, we don't need to be talking about this during Tali's birthday party." Greer glared at her mother.

My father, courageously, attempted to change the topic while we ate our salad. Then Jules brought in the huge platter of chicken francese. Cap followed with a family sized bowl of homemade pasta and all that delicious food kept conversation at a minimum.

We finished dinner and then came the stunning seven layer cakes, covered in a dark chocolate ganache. I did the honor of cutting larges slices for everyone and then we began to eat.

"Are we going to sing Happy Birthday?" Victoria asked.

"I hate that song," I replied.

Fitch laughed. "This is just like home."

"Your family or mine?" Kerwin asked.

"Dad," Kate began. "We're all one family now. It's been over thirty years."

She was beautiful now. I couldn't imagine what she looked like when Cam's father met her.

How fortunate for Cam to have both his parents with him.

"When do we open presents? Tomorrow?" Victoria asked.

"Open the damn thing," Greer said across the table.

I felt Lockie's knee against mine as I reached for the box and opened it. Lifting the lid, I could see a gold circus horse pin encrusted with tiny green stones.

"Thank you, Victoria, that was very thoughtful of you."

"Where are all the other presents," she asked.

"I'm not that into presents," I replied.

"Your father could buy you nearly anything," Victoria said.

"The point isn't to buy something, it's to do something," I explained knowing it was a concept well beyond her ken.

"We all did something," my father started, "in that we chipped in to get something that was doing something."

I looked from Greer to Jules who was smiling her bright smile.

Greer got up from the table and went to the hall closet while Lockie cleared a large space on the table. She returned with a large box and placed it in front of me.

"Happy Birthday, Tal."

"Do you have an idea what it is," Victoria asked.

"No, she doesn't know. It's a surprise," Greer snapped.

"You always knew what you were getting."

"That's because you always asked me."

"Maybe you asked her."

"Talia doesn't want anything," Greer said.

After getting the ribbon and the paper off, Jules took those away and I opened the lid. It was something silver. As big as a coffee urn.

"You'll have to take it out of the box," Lockie told me.

He held the box while I lifted it out.

It was a trophy.

My eyes filled with tears and my throat closed.

"Miry Brook Hunt Club," Jules read the engraving. "Sarah Rose Margolin Memorial Award."

"It was Greer's idea to create a championship in your mother's honor," my father said.

"Thank you," I managed to say. "Would it be rude if I left my party now?"

"You're the birthday girl," Jules replied. "You get to do whatever you like."

I kissed Jules, then went around the table to kiss Greer, my grandparents and my father. "Thank you. My mother would have appreciated this very much."

Lockie and I left. I cried all the way to the carriage house, but that wasn't very far.

"So you had a good birthday, Tal?" Lockie asked as we entered the house.

I put my arms around him. "Yes. It will be wonderful for the trophy to be a permanent fixture at the hunt club, engraved with the winners' names, into the future. People won't know who she was but at least they'll know her name. A few people."

"You can give her biography in the prize list. Write about her good works and hope she inspires them the way she inspired you."

"That was so thoughtful of Greer."

"That's not the Greer who greeted me when I arrived."

"No, it's not."

"Talia, I need to have a serious talk with you. Would you like to do it now or tomorrow?"

"Are you leaving?"

"I said I would stay until you get tired of me and I mean it. Tonight might be that night."

"Is this something that's been on your mind for a while?"

Lockie stepped away from me. "Yeah, but how did you know that?"

"I know you. Whatever it is, spit it out and we can go upstairs."

"You might not want to."

"I guarantee I do."

Lockie walked to his desk and switched on the small lamp. "There's...when I took this job, your father asked certain things of me, like not to have sexual relations with either of you before you were eighteen. That was actually pretty easy, especially in Greer's case. We know what happened in Florida. Your father really had it right."

"Lockie, please, just say it."

"It seems like now is the perfect time to start being sexually active. You're eighteen. You probably thought it would have happened by now."

"Not really."

"I've been trying to figure out how to explain this to you...I dated Jennifer."

"Yes," I replied.

"I was not celibate when I was on the circuit. A straight male has every option available and I wasn't a slacker in that regard. Then I met Jennifer and were together a lot."

"It was serious," I said.

"That's going too far. It was between a one-night stand and going steady. She has good qualities and I enjoyed being with her. She's fun. She's a good jumper rider. Fearless. A little too much so but she was moving in the same circle I was, so it was very convenient." Lockie paused.

"Do you want to go back to her? If you do, that's fine. Tell me before you do it."

"Talia, she killed my baby, I never want to see her again."

"She got pregnant?"

"She got pregnant and one day between classes, she went to a doctor and had my child terminated. I wasn't asked, I wasn't told. My child. My son who would have looked like me and grown up to be a fantastic event rider. Or my daughter who would have gotten a pony, and wore her hair in braids like your Glitter Girls do. Who would have giggled when I teased her. That child is dead. I would have found a way to raise it. I would have hired a nanny, changed my life, whatever it took. It was my child. But I wasn't asked. It wasn't any of my business."

"Lockie, I'm so sorry."

"I can't take that risk again because birth control obvious fails as proven by Jennifer Nicholson."

"As proven by my mother," I replied.

"I don't want to compare Jennifer with your mother in any way."

"I know what happened because she told me. I know there was a failure of science but I know they loved each other and loved me. It was hard for them."

"Did you mother consider getting rid of you before—"

"No. Babies are gifts not burdens or punishments."

"At dinner I watched Cam's parents. When they met, Kate was your age. They got married. They've been together thirty years. Sometimes I think that was a different world. Maybe you could marry your first love then and stay together. Maybe today you can't do that."

"This is why all that replacement boyfriend talk kept coming up. You think I don't have enough experience to know how I feel about you."

"I think what you feel for me is real. But neither of us know if it's lasting. Talia, say we went that next step. What if you had a baby and then we broke up. What if you didn't want me in your life or my child's life? Do you think I could survive that?"

"You have to...did she tell you this the day before your accident?"

"This isn't a movie! I didn't get on Wing, upset, lacking concentration, thinking about the bitch Jennifer and crash into the fence. The mud was deep, he lost his footing and I took a bad fall."

I looked at him.

"I did go to Germany shortly after she told me," Lockie admitted. "I would have gone to the moon to get away from her. Then she turned up at Acadiana again. I told Teche if he welcomed her back, consider me gone."

"So this happened three or four years ago."

Lockie nodded.

"What do you want to do?"

"I want to stay here forever but I think someday you will get tired of me. There will always be incidents like the one a few weeks ago where you took me to the hospital. I will always have headaches. I will always forget things I should remember, and I will never be a fun boyfriend."

"Missing square dances and the movies because they're too loud and going out at night isn't easy because the lights are too bright."

"Yeah. You deserve more than that."

"You wanted a choice and Jennifer didn't give it to you, right?"

"Right."

"Do I get a choice? Can I skip the square dances and choose to be with you? Or am I too young and inexperienced to know that? Are you going to treat me like Jennifer treated you, or are you going to trust me?"

"I don't have that much to give you."

"Criminey!" I headed for the stairs. "Can I be the judge of that?"

He followed me up the stairs.

"I don't want you to regret this choice."

"Will you please just take your shower so we can go to sleep?" I started pulling my braid out.

Lockie went into the bathroom, then came back into the bedroom. "You think you know your mind—"

"I know my mind and I know yours. Try to remember that I'm remembering for both of us now."

"You'll get tired of that."

"I'm counting to ten. If you don't get in the shower, I'll drag you into the wash stall. One. Two—"

"Silly, will you be here when I get out of the shower?"

"I live here. Where am I going to go?

His lips caressed mine so tenderly that I knew sometimes you just get lucky and find the right one the first time.

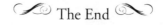 The End

If you love a book, tell a friend.

Sign up for our mailing list and be among the first to know when the next Bittersweet Farm book is released. Send your email address to: barbara@barbaramorgenroth.com

Note: All email addresses are strictly confidential and used only to notify of new releases.

About the Author

Barbara got her first horse, Country Squire, when she was eleven years old and considers herself lucky to have spent at least as much time on him as she did in the dirt. Next came Yankee Doodle who was far more cooperative and patient with her. Over the years, she showed in equitation classes, hunter classes, went on hunter paces, taught horseback riding at her stable called Sunshine Farm, and went fox hunting on an Appaloosa who would jump anything. With her Dutch Warmblood, Barbara began eventing and again found herself on a horse with great patience and who definitely taught her everything important she knows about horses.

Made in the USA
San Bernardino, CA
21 January 2015